AMONG HIS PERSONAL EFFECTS

AMONG HIS
PERSONAL EFFECTS

JOHN CRAIG MCDONALD

OAKTARA

WATERFORD, VIRGINIA

Among His Personal Effects

Published in the U.S. by:

OakTara Publishers
P.O. Box 8
Waterford, VA 20197

Visit OakTara at
www.oaktara.com

Cover design by David LaPlaca/debest design co.

Cover illustration of the Venerable Bede, compliments of
http://courses.ats.rochester.edu/hahn/eng150/ms-bede.jpg

Author photo © 2007 by David Wood.

ISBN: 978-1-60290-020-2

Among His Personal Effects is a work of fiction. References to real people, events,
establishments, organizations, or locales are intended only to provide a sense of
authenticity and are used fictitiously. All other characters, incidents, and dialogue are
drawn from the author's imagination.

Preface

This is a work of historical fiction. There was indeed a Robert Henryson, and he was a poet in the 15th century. The poetry that you will find in the story is a lightly modernized and sometimes slightly edited version of his real work. Although we know little of his life, there is a long tradition that he was also a schoolmaster at the abbey school of Dunfermline. One can make a good case that he received training in canon (church) and civil law. He died, according to one story, from the flux.

It is also true that in the summer of 1482, certain members in the court of James III were hanged by disgruntled nobles at a bridge in the Border town of Lauder. Some scholars have argued that Henryson's adaptation of Aesop's fables grew out of his reflection on this and other events from a deeply troubled time in Scotland's history. Archbishop Scheves and Archibald, 6th Earl of Angus, were also historical persons; and there were Crichtons who were abbots of Dunfermline Abbey. These people and events provide the framework for the present novel.

By far the largest element of the work, however, is fictional. Henryson's students and his connection with the hangings at Lauder, as well as some of the relationships between historical characters are purely the figment of my imagination.

Those wishing to read Henryson's poetry in the Middle Scots (a challenge, but not impossible, even without training) might look to *The Poems of Robert Henryson*, TEAMS Middle English Texts, Western Michigan University, 1997. A good introduction to the period is *The Edinburgh History of Scotland Vol. 2: The Later Middle Ages* by Ranald Nicholson, New Edition, Hyperion Books, 1986. I have taken the liberty to put in the mouth of John de Leith (my fictional secretary to the Earl of Angus) words belonging to David Hume of Godscroft, a later chronicler of the Angus family. This fascinating story of one of the great noble houses in Scotland may be found in *The History of the House of Angus*, edited by David Reid and published by the Scottish Text Society in two volumes, 2005.

There are a number of people I wish to thank. For reading earlier drafts of the work and for their comments and support: my parents, John and Aileen McDonald, and my sister, Laura Drummond; my father-in-law, Reg Murphy; and my son-in-law, Justin Reynolds. I am grateful to Lila Ray, formerly reference librarian at King College, and to Jean Bane, formerly of

King College, for their friendly aid as I was researching this period. When completing my dissertation on Henryson many years ago, my brother Bruce offered some words of encouragement I will always hold dear.

Special thanks are due to my literary companions—The Penheads—during the writing of this novel. Tommy Bryant, Andy Simoson, Brandon Story, and Chuck Thompson suffered through the halting conception of the work and patiently read draft after tentative draft. The story would have suffered greatly without their advice and encouragement. Thank you, my friends.

I would like to express my love for my wife, Karen, and for my children, Kate and Seth, with thanks to them, partly for their patient company to Scottish monasteries and castles, but more importantly for a life out of which this novel grows.

To Ramona Tucker and Jeff Nesbit of OakTara I am grateful for seeing this story to publication with such courtesy and forbearance. It has been a pleasure working with them.

Ultimately, this book is about a teacher and his students, from any time or place. Although there is no resemblance between the characters in the novel and persons now living, it certainly would have been poorer but for the privilege of teaching alongside my friends and colleagues at King College. I must especially acknowledge the great debt I owe to my students of the past quarter century. A number of them have become part of the fabric of my life. This novel is really for them.

Deo Gloria

JOHN CRAIG MCDONALD
King College

I

The Preaching of the Swallow

The old man laid down his quill. Until this moment, he had been furiously scratching with it on the parchment before him. From somewhere under his trundle bed, he heard another scratching, like an echo of his own, but fainter. He smiled.

"A family you'll be having, then, is it?" He spoke to a pair of whiskers quivering in the shadows over a bit of cheese. "You'll be wanting to move them to safety. I'll not be able to feed and harbor you much longer, especially with your wee bairns. You'd best be on." The old man stretched his arms and rubbed his eyes, but his movements did nothing to faze the hungry mouse. "Right then. Suit yourself. I'll do what I can while I can. But you've been warned."

Robert was dying. He knew that even before the abbey's herbalist had run through the list of concoctions to stop the flux that now filled his chamber pot each night with the foul-smelling brown soup tinged with red. Even before Father Charles, the cellarer and his confessor for all these years, took hold of his wasted arms with those massive hands, and said, with tears in his eyes, "Well, my old friend, it's time to order your affairs, do you not think? I'll be wanting to instruct you on how to prepare my own cell in the new kingdom, next to your own." The broad smile parted that great beard as it had done so many times before, though the teeth were fewer and yellow and though the whiskers were now completely gray.

It was for this reason—his dying—that Robert was writing so late in the twilight of the Dunfermline summer, long after compline, when the monks had retired to their cells. It was for this reason, in the stillness of the great abbey in the heart of this royal burgh all enveloped in sleep, he could hear the rustling of the mice.

❖

His bowels rumbled sharply and suddenly. He lifted the lid of the pot and squatted to expel yet more of his life. Death's insistence pressed him to work on, though he would gladly lie down. "Just a wee while longer," he whispered to God's grim messenger. "Another day or two, and I'll be finished. Then you can have your way with me."

Returning to his desk, Robert wrote for some hour or so until his eyes grew too weary to struggle with the dying twilight. He extinguished the candle at his desk and felt his way to his bed in the dark. He sat down heavily. Although he was desperately weary, sleeping seemed like a luxury. There would be an eternity enough for rest. Besides, his mind would not keep still, agitating the memories that lodged there. "How strange," he mused, "that the spirit should move about so at the very time the body would be still." This thought itself convinced him of St. Paul's truth: there had to be a new body strong enough to house such an active spirit. Another rumbling in his bowels prompted him to pray that his body in the resurrection would not have an arse-hole. While at the university, during the frequent *disputationes quodlibet*, he had heard the masters debate whether Adam had a navel. At this moment, he would eagerly have learned their conclusions on this more pressing matter.

"Patience, my man," he admonished himself. "The Lord'll be knowing your need." The rumbling passed without event, and his memories turned to a winter feast at Stirling Castle in 1481 and to the months that followed and to the people who moved in those times. Such memories seldom left him now.

He had occasionally wondered if it had been his pride that was responsible for all that happened. Had others been punished for his great sin? Charles had assured him that this was not so. Each had made his choice. And, as he was later to learn, another had made her choice. Still, he couldn't help wondering. He little repented of his pride that evening. What man wouldn't? Here were three of his own pupils: Ingram Bannatyne, assistant choral master to William Roger, the royal musician; John de Leith, personal secretary to Archibald Douglas, the Earl of Angus, arguably Scotland's greatest magnate; and George Crichton, Master of the Royal Entertainments and a groomsman of the King's wardrobe. Even now, these many years later, he warmed to the reflected glory he had felt that evening. They were his students, each remarkable in his own way, and he had determined that they would never be wanting for light to flourish in. That night he was to add a luster of his own. By command of Their Majesties, James and Margaret, he was to read his "Cresseid."

❧

The evening had begun with a high Mass and a sermon preached by the great Archbishop of St. Andrews himself. Stories about Archbishop Scheves abounded, few of them flattering. Together they depicted a man who was ambitious, politically astute, learned, cunning, impassive. Piety was seldom included as one of his virtues, if by that one meant a retiring, contemplative manner. He certainly made no attempt to pretend the virtue, either. There was little to endear the prelate, but one thing was certain: he commanded through his presence. Whatever his defects as a pastor, he was determined to preserve the integrity of the Church and the Crown in Scotland, each in its own sphere; and he had done so to the apparent satisfaction of both pope and king. In a word, he was antithetical to most everything Robert prized in a churchman, especially one in such authority, who had the power but no will to bring about spiritual renewal.

Appropriate to the day, the Feast of Childermas, Scheves took as his text the passage from the Gospel of Matthew detailing the Massacre of the Innocents. Through a series of verbal acrobatics, the good Archbishop leapt from Holy Scripture to Boethius' *De consolatione philosophiae* to speak of prudence, one of the four great cardinal virtues. *Rather cruel,* Robert thought. *Joseph and the Magi had the benefit of dreams to warn them of impending danger. The parents of those poor children in Bethlehem had no such divine aid. They could not foresee Herod's great anger and so suffered.*

The homily briefly summarized Boethius' teaching about the inability of man's limited reason, bound as it is by sensuality, to see God's high magnificence. With his deep, resonant voice, Scheves summoned the words as if by some incantation. "In his *Metaphysics* Aristotle says that man's soul is like a bat's eye that sleeps during the light of day, but in the gloaming comes forth to fly. Yet—" he paused for effect—"we may have knowledge of God by his creatures."

He illustrated with a fable about a wee swallow, who urges her companions to eat the linseed that the husbandman has scattered in the spring. "Otherwise," she argued, "when the crop grows to maturity, the husbandman will make nets by which to capture and destroy us." Failing to heed the warning, the birds later perish when the swallow's prophecy was fulfilled.

The moral of the sermon was conventional enough: this august congregation was being urged to measure carefully their actions as to future consequences, not just immediate results. The fable was also conveniently vague. To whom the farmer or the birds might refer could, at any moment, be anyone's guess. It was the character of such sermons, in the hands of a skilled orator, that the applications could refer to everyone and no one as the times indicated. It was clear, of course, that Scheves was the prophetic voice of the wee swallow. Robert wondered if the meaning were somehow bound up with the interview Scheves had had only that morning with the King.

Although Charles complained of Robert's dourness, there was in the poet's temperament a chronic perversity to laugh when men such as the archbishop spoke. They lumbered on, conscious of their own dignity, drawing attention to each rhetorical flourish, all the while providing Robert something other than what they intended. Little in Robert's experience was completely wasted; some kernel, however small, could always spring to life in most unexpected ways. Had he not said as much when in an idle moment he had written these lines?

> As through the stubborn ground,
> So it be tilled and plowed with great diligence,
> Spring up the flowers and the corn abounds,
> Wholesome and good to all men's sustenence,
> So does spring there a moral sweet sentence
> Out of the subtle song of poetry,
> To good purpose, who could it well apply.
>
> The walnut's shell, though it be hard and tough,
> Holds the kernel, sweet and delectable;
> So lies therein a doctrine wise enough
> And full of fruit, under a feignéd fable;
> And clerks tell us, it is right profitable
> In sad affairs to mingle merry sport,

To lighten hearts and cause the time be short.

Thus, while Scheves droned on, Robert lingered behind on the fable, breathing life into its dead bones. Robert's father himself was a husbandman, and well Robert knew the passing of the seasons: awaking to spring mornings aching and stiff from hours of guiding a plow through rocky soil, fervent prayers for rain as the crops were growing and for sun as the harvest drew nigh; the bitterness of the winters. The snow falling out in the gloomy courtyard reminded him all too keenly of those boyhood nights tending to sick animals. He shivered inadvertently.

But spring always followed. "Summer's secretary." Yes, that was the phrase. Lines began to form themselves.

> Summer's secretary with his seal,
> When columbine uprises through the clay,
> Which hardened was before with frosts so fell.

In his tale, he recalled those rare times when he had stolen a moment to pause from his work so as to drink in the aroma of the flowers, the tang of the manured ground ready to receive its seed, and the chatter of the mavis and other birds. He saw his father and the other laborers,

> Some making dykes, and some harnessing the plows,
> Some casting wide their seeds from place to place,
> The harrows hopping in the sowers' trace;
> It was great joy to him that loved the corn
> To see them labor, both at eve and morn.

And after stopping for shade under a hawthorn hedge, his boyhood image saw a flock of birds berated by a swallow:

> "See ye yon churl," said she, "beyond yon plow
> Fast sowing hemp—lo see!—also flaxseed?
> Yon lint will grow in little time indeed,
> And thereof will yon churl his strong nets make,
> For traps to set, by which he will us take.

> "Therefore I urge we pass when he is gone
> At even, and with our nails so sharp and small

5

Out of the earth scrape we yon seed anon
And eat it up, for if it grows we shall
Have cause to weep hereafter, one and all."

The other birds, however, ignored the swallow's warning to exercise
prudence, "as wise clerks say," and departed. As witness in his own story Robert then saw himself making his way for home, wondering at the
strangeness of his vision as if he had "seen a fairy." In summer he returned
to the same place and there again heard the swallow pleading with the
other birds.

"O blind birds, and full of negligence,
Unmindful of your own prosperity,
Lift up your sight and take good advisement,
Look to the lint that grows upon yon lea!
Yon is the thing I warned, forsooth, that we,
While it was seed, should root forth off the earth:
Now is it lint; now is it large in girth.

"Go yet, while it is tender, young, and small,
And pull it up, let it no more increase!
My flesh grows weak, my body trembles all,
Thinking on it I may not sleep in peace!"

Again, the birds ignored the swallow's advice, more urgent now; and
Robert could well imagine the husbandman cultivating the flax and his
wife flailing it and spinning it to make the coarse thread for clothing or net-
ting. He had seen his own father and mother do the same so many times;
and when he and his brother and sister had grown old enough, they joined
in the task.

Then to Robert's memory came the Border winters, with the wind
blowing both sleet and hedge almost at the horizontal. The flock of birds
returned, looking in vain for food; and he, the storyteller, cried to see the
farmer strike them with his staff, breaking their necks or heads, or stuff
some, while still alive, in his poke.

In the face of such tragedy the swallow offered only this conclusion:

"Lo," said she, "it happens that advice
Is lost on such as these. Will counsel they not heed

Of prudent men or clerks accounted wise?"

All such tales demanded an appropriate interpretation—*moralitas*, as Robert informed his boys—which made clear the tropological or moral lesson. Robert decided to assign to the husbandman the part of the devil (with a wry prayer of apology to the soul of his dead father), to the wee birds the benighted souls, and to the swallow the preacher.

"*In nomine patri, filii, et spiritu sancti, amen.*" With this benediction, the fable vanished. Robert felt a sudden chill and crossed himself. Alone in his bedchamber that night he would make notes from which to fashion his story later. "*Pax vobiscum,*" the archbishop intoned. The service had moved to the Eucharist.

Robert did jot down the notes to his story, but it was not until these last weeks of his life that he wove them into finished cloth. Whatever Scheves might have meant by the fable then lay with him in his grave some seven years since. And if anyone in the congregation had bothered to take Scheves' words to heart, it was likely that he or she, too, was dead. But in the light of events that followed in the next spring and summer, a special meaning had forced itself on Robert, with prophetic urgency, because it was his boys who were the small fowls, though they little knew it. The rich feast thrown their way on Childermas was simply bait for the cruel farmer's trap.

What a trap it was. Fate had gone to elaborate means to lull all of them to sleep in her bosom. After Mass, the large party adjourned to the Great Hall, which had only recently been refurbished by Thomas Cochrane, the chief mason. Such was the royal esteem that Cochrane had been appointed chancellor of the realm. It was an achievement unparalleled in any of the chronicles, that a man of such common birth should rise to a position normally held by a magnate or a prince of the Church. Cochrane was determined that the feast should express his gratitude and his expensive tastes. Wines were imported from Germany, Spain, Portugal, Italy, and France to satisfy even the most discriminating palate. Dishes of capon, goose, mutton, salmon, herring, and eel stew burdened the tables. Gamekeepers had just the day before brought in wagons of venison and grouse.

Robert was hosted by George Crichton, who traced the story of how the "Cresseid" had reached the royal notice. "You commissioned a certain bookseller to produce a faircopy of it, did you not?" George's tone was conspiratorial.

"From Isaac Abercrombie, aye. He's been the abbey's procurer of books for many a decade."

"'Procurer.' Uhm, a suitable turn of phrase. Most suitable, indeed." George seemed to savor the word.

"What do you mean?" Robert asked.

George winked. "For a small retainer he informs me of works he considers worthy of performance. You can imagine my delight when he informed me of your 'Cresseid.' There was a delicious irony in his being the Pandarus to your wanton."

"It had been no wanton were he simply to have copied it as I asked."

George delighted to see his former schoolmaster struggling between anger and pleasure. He also delighted in intensifying the struggle. "O, he copied it, all right. Three times, as it turned out."

"Three? That old wretch."

"One copy for you, one for me, and, when she saw how taken I was with it, one for the Queen."

"The Queen?"

"Aye. I showed it to her. She has exquisite taste, you know. I was all ready to invite you for the spring, but she approached me first. She would wait no longer than the Christmas season."

Robert's anger, never great to begin with, surrendered unconditionally, and pleasure took sole possession of the field. And so the meal continued, as George, Ingram, and John, in turn, welcomed him. After the servants cleared the boards of their remnants and replenished the cups and tankards, George led the poet/schoolmaster to the stage and announced: "Your Royal Majesties, Master Robert Henryson of Dunfermline." He added, "Our Scottish Chaucer," and turned long enough for Robert to catch a glimpse of that faint familiar smile.

II

The Testament of Cresseid

Despite the churning in his mind, sitting up was too great an effort, and Robert lay down on his bed. The mouse family below moved about in annoyance. In the silence, the rustling was loud enough to have kept him awake. In former days, he, too, would have been annoyed. But not tonight. He took comfort in their presence.

The sound of the mice attempting to settle reminded Robert of the stirring of his audience that evening: the scraping of benches on the stone floor, the clanking of goblets after one last draft of wine, the soft hissing of the garments shaping themselves around bodies searching to find comfort.

Even now, sick old man that he was, Robert still felt that nervousness that had hollowed out his stomach that evening. He had tried to hide the blush that threatened to envelop his whole face, by leaning over and pretending to arrange with painstaking care his manuscript. He stalled for yet more time by taking a sip from his tankard. Then, clearing his throat, he had looked up.

✣

The hall grew silent, and in the silence he realized his fright. It was one thing to imagine reading before the court. Little else had been in Robert's thoughts for the previous three months, ever since he had received the invitation. And he had practiced on the patient ear of Father Charles, who swore that he didn't mind hearing the story read for a fifth and sixth time. Charles, however, was but an audience of one and was not the king. Around Robert tonight sat the glory of Scotland, the lords temporal and spiritual.

Robert fought against the trembling that would betray his nervousness, thankful for the heavy winter's gown that the boisterous December had foisted upon him. The shaking would not be seen. But the cloak could not hide the tremor in his voice, and he began tentatively.

> A doleful season to some weighty verse
> Should correspond and be equivalent.
> Right so it was when I sought to rehearse
> This tragedy. The weather right fervent,
> When Aries, in the middle part of Lent,
> Hail showers began from the north descend,
> That scarcely from the cold I might defend.

Members of the audience shifted in their seats; cloaks rustled. Robert strove to assume a confidence he did not feel.

> Though love be hot, yet in a man of age
> It kindles not so soon as in his youth,
> In whom the blood is flowing in a rage.
> In ancient men, whose fervor drags and droops,
> Against the cold a fire provides best proof,
> To help by physic where nature has failed.
> I am expert, for both I have assailed.

Some encouraging laughter in the audience, and it was as if Robert was transported back to his classroom, regaling his boys to stories and fables to illustrate some theological or moral point. He became the old man whom love had deserted. He raised his tankard for effect.

> I stirred the fire, and puttered me about,
> Then took a drink my spirits to comfort,
> And armed me well from freezing cold there-out.

10

> To cut the winter night, and make it short,
> I took a book, and left all other sport,
> Written be worthy Chaucer glorious,
> Of fair Cresseid and lusty Troilus.

To while away the hours, the forlorn narrator pulled another book off his shelf, one that disputed Chaucer's telling of the story and dared challenge the master with these words: "Who knows if all that Chaucer wrote was true?" In this version of the story, the beautiful Cresseid, who had forsaken the Trojan prince Troilus, found herself cast off by her new lover, the Greek hero Diomedes. She was left to become, as "some men say," a courtesan. Robert sought to capture the old man's anguished defense of the guilty woman who had charmed him with her fictional beauty.

> O, fair Cresseid! The flower and *A per se*
> Of Troy and Greece, how wast thou fortunate!
> To change to filth thy femininity,
> And be with fleshly lust so maculate.

> Yet nevertheless, whatever men think or say,
> In scornful language of thy faithlessness,
> I shall excuse, as far forth as I may,
> Thy womanhood, thy wisdom, and fairness;
> The which Fortune has put to such distress
> As her pleases, and no thing through the guilt
> Of thee, through wicked language to be spoiled.

No amount of pleading, however, could evoke pity in the gods, who chafed under Cresseid's accusation that Venus and Cupid had betrayed her. In solemn convocation they passed judgment on her and sentenced her in a way that would strike at the heart of her identity: her beauty.

To carry out the "sentence definitive" the gods chose one intimately familiar with disease—Mercury, the heavenly physician, "clad in a scarlet gown and furred well, as such a one ought to be." He passed this doom:

> "From health of body I thee now deprive,
> And to thy sickness there shall be no cure,
> But in dolor all thy days to endure."

While writing the next portion of his tale, Robert had drawn on the numerous times he had been accosted by lepers waiting by the abbey precinct, hoping for some charity by the abbot or his bursar. As he described the terrible transformation in his heroine, he could sense in his audience the shudder he had felt when he first wrote the words.

> "Thy crystal eyes mingled with blood I make,
> Thy voice so clear, unpleasing, harsh, and hoarse,
> Thy fair complexion spoiled with cankers black,
> And swollen lump appearing in thy face;
> Where'er thou come each man shall flee the place.
> Thus shall thou go begging from house to house,
> With cup and clapper like a lazarus."

Now a social outcast, Cresseid was delivered to the leper house where she was to spend the rest of her days. There she railed against a fortune that was even more crushing than before. Gone were her ornate tapestries and soft bed, her silks and golden hairpins, her fine wine, her golden cups, her gardens, her music, her fair attendants. All this she had exchanged for a bunch of straw, molded bread, and sour cider.

Chided by a fellow leper to make a virtue of necessity, since weeping only doubled one's woe, Cresseid learned the law of leper folk and shuffled with them from place to place to fight off the hunger and the cold. To noble passers-by they shook their cups and shouted: "Worthy lords, for God's love of Heaven, to us poor lepers impart your alms deed."

It was then that the noble Troilus rode by. He did not recognize Cresseid, but the leper standing before him brought to mind his former love, and he bestowed on the wretched creature a great sum in her memory. Likewise, Cresseid, who was blinded by her disease, did not recognize her benefactor and learned his identity only after he left. For the first time in the story, she placed the blame fully on herself, acknowledging Troilus' magananimity and her own infidelity.

Cresseid ended her woeful story with her testament, bequeathing her corpse to the worms and her cup and clapper, along with all her gold, to the other leper folk. To Troilus, she left her "royal ring, set with this ruby red," which he had sent to her in his own grief at her betrayal.

Troilus, for his part, built a "tomb of marble gray," and inscribed these words on it:

Lo, fair ladies, Cresseid of Troy's town,
One time counted the flower of womanhood,
Under this stone, late a leper, lies dead.

When Robert finished reading, no one spoke or moved. After an embarrassing moment, he gathered his manuscript, staring down all the while. In his shame he longed to make a hasty retreat. It was then that he heard the quiet and thoughtful clapping of a single person. He looked up in the direction from which it came. It was Queen Margaret. There were tears in her eyes. Robert bowed solemnly to her and allowed George to escort him back to his seat. By this time, the rest of the court had joined the queen in her applause.

Later that night, while lying on his bed waiting for sleep, he recounted the evening. True, he had not been borne aloft by great winds of adulation. In this he felt some pain, though the kind words and reasoned praise of George, Ingram, and John had tempered his disappointment. But the greatest praise was the queen's real tears, drawn forth by tears his quill had shaped. This was ample reward. Sleep did eventually find him and pronounced him content.

The next morning, the queen's page brought a pouch containing ten merks and a letter from her majesty, written in her own halting hand. He led Robert to the stable, where his mule was waiting for him, saddled and bridled. From the Chapel Royal came the distant strains of chanting.

"The King attends Mass early," Robert spoke, more to himself, but the page answered.

"Aye. He'll be hunting this morning."

Because the main gate was not yet open, Robert exited by the postern on the east side of the burgh. The protection of the wall had deceived him about the strength of the wind. Once outside, he drew his cloak tightly about him to protect himself from its blast. Still, he was eager to read the queen's words, so he drew his mule to a stop and turned it around so his back was to the wind. He withdrew the letter from the bag and broke the seal. The wind tore at the parchment in an effort to free it from his hands, and sleet dampened it in places. He persisted. The queen commended his verse to the favor of the world and his soul to the mercy of Jesu. When he turned back to face the wind, his eyes were wet, and not only from sleet. It was the last time he ever saw her.

✣

The memory paused. *If life had only stopped there,* the old Robert thought. Had that moment been his last, he would have died a happy man. But though he could pause the memory, he could not stop it altogether. It began to move again.

Having folded the queen's letter carefully, he observed a party of lepers in the dreamy morning twilight like a dark cloud. A hospital, only recently endowed, lay in his direction. The lepers were making their way in the early light, huddled together against the weather, to the southern road leading to Edinburgh, where they were licensed to beg for their sustenance. When they saw him emerge, they beat their clappers and thrust toward him a small thicket of rods, to which were attached pouches. Charity might thus be offered without risk of infection. He fumbled in the purse that the queen's page had given him, but his cowl beat about his eyes in the wind. He brushed it back from his head.

"To be divided among you all." He placed in the nearest of the pouches a merk, a tithe of his gift from the queen. The coin, two thirds of a pound Scots, was a king's ransom to such as these. He felt in some way indebted to them. Hadn't his Cresseid, after all, been one of their kind? Hadn't he drawn the details of her affliction from observing their own?

A hoarse choir blessed him in the howling storm. He pulled up his hood and turned his mule to go; but as he did so, he heard one voice among the rest: "Jesu bless you, Master Robert Henryson." He turned about in his saddle to eye the leper flock. Like him, they had all bundled up against the cold, and the speaker could not, or would not, be identified. At the time he had wondered whether his cowl had perhaps muffled part of the benediction laid upon him. Perhaps it was only his imagination. Perhaps it was the wind. Whatever confusion he had felt then, Robert now knew, in these his dying hours, that the voice sounded the first click of Fortune's wheel past her highest point.

III

The Fox, the Wolf, and the Husbandman

At last the mice settled down, but still Robert could not sleep. Not just yet. He stared up into the darkness. If Fortune had catapulted him past the highest point of her wheel so many years ago, logic would dictate that she had raised him to the top in the first place. So when had the movement upward begun?

In the life of a husbandman's family, one like Robert's own, Fortune's wheel seldom moved at all, unless it were downwards. In fact, it was less a wheel than a bucket that had become untied from its winch above a great well. Had events run their normal course, he would have followed his father, Joshua, as a plowman in the Borders. He recalled that voice booming across the dales, commanding the unruly oxen to order: "How! Haik! Hold draft, my doves" and of the angry pledge that the wolf "might have you all at once!"

Joined with the stubborn oxen were early risings, crippling toil, plain fare, dreamless sleeps. Marriage, bairns, burials. Each of these moments ticking away a largely unnoticed existence.

Largely, but not entirely unnoticed. There was always a wolf lurking nearby to hear the plowman's rantings, eager to take him up on his rash oath. In the Henryson family, the wolf was the English or Scottish reiver. When carrying out their depredations on one another, such marauders noticed only too well the ripe fields and pillaged them, either to put food into their famished wombs or to prevent their enemies from doing so. Twice they had plundered the Henryson lands. Fortunately just twice, some might say. But for a man of Henryson's small means, Nature herself was an opponent formidable enough to wrest a living from. She did not need assistance.

Plunder came to the Border farmer in many guises. Enter the fox, the abbot of Kelso, whose lands Joshua Henryson held in feu ferm. The abbot had grand designs to renovate the abbey church for the glory of God and had sent out a decree that all his little world was to be taxed. It took no lawyer—civil or canon—to see the paradox. Even the eight-year-old Robert suspected that there was something vastly unfair in his father's having to pay for something the abbot would receive glory for, on this earth and in the hereafter. But such was the way of the world. The law turned a blind eye, but it was not the blind eye of justice. The elder Henryson had appealed the taxation to the consistory court after the marauders had come that spring. Affairs of crown and baron little occupied the archdeacon, who was more likely to see in the depredations God's hand of judgment on a profane husbandman, and so let the assessment stand.

Partly to curb the severity of the abbot's vengeance, but more to spare his son a life of rural misery, Joshua offered young Robert to the service of Mother Church. If oppression were the natural order of things, better his son benefit from it than suffer its ravages. Such was the thinking of a simple farmer who could seldom look beyond two evil alternatives.

Although his course had been determined by others, Robert set upon it eagerly and with some success. He was admitted as a pauper scholar to the newly established university in Glasgow. His studies, however, were interrupted by the death of his father. What the reivers and the abbot of Kelso could not do to the plowman, Nature did. She broke him. He caught a chill when trying to save a harvest from an unexpected rain. He could save neither his crop nor his health.

To support his mother and younger siblings, Robert resigned himself to tutoring Malcolm and Samuel, the sons of Alexander Inglis—a prosperous merchant of Edinburgh—and his wife Catherine. Alexander was a forward-thinking man, who realized how much greater a help and how much more pleasant a companion his wife might have been to him had she had even the most elementary learning; so he encouraged young Isabel, his daughter of fourteen years, to sit in on the lessons of her older brothers. She needed little encouragement. The most apt of the three children, she had also developed a young maiden's fancy for the young man, who tried to convince himself that hers was a pure eagerness, but who also felt a mixed pleasure in her attentions. The spirit of resignation slowly disappeared.

Robert didn't know when it happened, when his affection for Isabel took that dangerous turn. It had certainly not been love at first sight. She was old enough to be contracted in marriage, but not yet mature enough to entangle the heart of a university man like himself. Though a pupil in her mother's school when he released her from his, Isabel still wore a woman's ways like an ill-fitting gown, cut too full in some places, too long in others, tripping her up when most she wished to impress. Her mother had unlocked an armory of weapons—the bashful smile, the coy downward glance, the flippant toss of her head, the mincing step—and each of these weapons Isabel tested on her tutor. She was too unskilled, too awkward and clumsy in their use even to dent his armor, much less pierce it. Besides, he was safe, more of a target to practice on than an armed foe. Or so one might have thought. But there were hints of other things. As a girl, Isabel wanted his admiration; as a woman, she wanted his affection.

For Robert's own part, Isabel was, at first, little more to him than his sister Alice, who was nearly her same age. Like Alice, she was the source of amusement and annoyance and wonder. Amusement in her gawky ways, caught between childhood and womanhood. Knocking over her tankard while reaching daintily for the bread, turning her ankle on the stairs while trying to enter a room grandly, getting caught up in a tussle with her two brothers when decorum ordered that she should maintain composure and indifference. Annoyance that the moon threw into such disarray her moods each month. And wonder during those moments when she was least self-conscious, unaware that he might be staring at her. When bent over her tablet in concentration, she chewed reflectively on her stylus or brushed errant strands of hair from her eyes.

The change could not have come instantaneously, he thought, but he could at least mark the point when he was first aware of it, when his armor was already pierced and he was already wounded.

She had not been sixteen yet two months when it became clear that her father had destined her to be the spouse of Edward Crichton, the fourteen-year-old son of Lord Crichton. The match had value for both sides. The Inglises obviously profited by allying themselves to a noble family, albeit one whose luster was less brilliant than in earlier times. The Crichtons, for their part, would add the merchant's wealth to their land-poor coffers without sacrificing too great a blow to their noble stature. Edward, after all, was the third son. More profitable, prestigious marriages had been arranged for his older brothers.

The Inglises were to be the guests of the Crichtons for a week at Crichton Castle, some short distance south of Edinburgh. There the young people could meet one another and the contract of betrothal could be drawn up. Robert would accompany the family so that the studies of the Inglis children might continue. It was while at the banquet, when Isabel entered the hall to be introduced to Edward, that he noticed for the first time the transformation that had been taking place in her. The gown had been cut so as to display to their best advantage the delicate breasts that would, in all probability, never grow much beyond this their maiden state; her hair had been arranged so as to soften the angular features of her face. She was escorted by her father; and her arm rested on his with all the gentleness and lightness of some butterfly poised to take flight again. Gone was her coy bashfulness. She looked steadily ahead at the Crichton table, where her husband-to-be sat. All awkwardness had disappeared.

"My Lord and Lady Crichton, Edward, please allow me to introduce my daughter, Isabel." Edward, who stood at Isabel's arrival, bowed with all the stiff formality he could manage at his age. Isabel curtsied and joined him at the table. During rare moments when his dinner companion, the elderly aunt of Lady Crichton, paused long enough in her harangue on the moral laxity of this present age to fill her mouth with stewed beef or a leg of mutton, Robert studied the young couple. Isabel was plainly miserable. Despite her efforts to engage young Edward in conversation, he seemed unwilling to return more than a nod or shake of his head.

Edward's lack of enthusiasm could have been that her looks failed to please him. True, she was not the beauty of some young women in the hall, nor would she ever be. But she was not unpleasant to look at. Perhaps, then, he was shy and immature. There was one last possibility. He was simply oafish, the product of indulgence and neglect. Whatever the cause, Isabel's refinements were, for the moment, wasted. Perhaps in time the quality of her spirit and mind would impress themselves upon him. How long that might be, however, Robert could not guess.

As the week wore on, it was apparent that Edward's behavior was not going to change. He seemed more eager to sport with Samuel and Malcolm than to court Isabel. Although mindful at all times of his superior rank and willing to invoke that superiority when the moment occasioned, he nevertheless won the hearts of the Inglis boys by taking them on horseback tours of the vast Crichton lands or by hunting coney with them. Isabel accompanied them, but was always relegated to the party of Crichton sisters and female cousins.

One morning, toward the end of the visit, when she had not been invited to join the hunting party, Robert approached her chamber at the instigation of mother Catherine Inglis, who sought the schoolmaster's aid in fortifying the young Isabel in the remembrance of her duty. He came armed with books for the purpose. When he knocked, she called out, "Who is it?"

"Master Henryson, Miss Isabel."

"Come in, please." Her courtesy sounded more like a plea for help. She was sitting at her writing desk alone, and it was obvious to him that she had been crying.

"Master Robert."

"Shall I get your mother?"

"No. She'll not understand. She'd only be ashamed of me."

Robert laid his books down and sat opposite to her. "Why is that?"

"Can you not see?"

"It's Edward, you mean?"

"Aye. He's more interested in hunting with Samuel and Malcolm."

Robert felt his heart race, but he knew his position. "He's young yet, no more than a lad. In time he'll come around, I've no doubt."

Isabel grabbed for Robert's arm in desperation. "I cannot love him."

Robert struggled in his own desperation not to take that hand. He turned to his authorities for refuge. " *Cannot* is an over-strong word. Have you forgotten the distinction between *can* and *will*? Where's my scholar? If it's *cannot* you'll be speaking about, then you must know that it's our fortune that can never bring about our happiness. But if you will not love Edward, that's a different matter. Boethius found consolation in the wisdom of Dame Philosophy."

"Console me not with the consolations of an old man who had good fortune to lose. I've not had my chance."

"Aye, but his argument holds nonetheless. Only by subjecting our will to reason might we find true happiness."

"But it's not my reason." Isabel clinched her fists and struck the desk.

Robert could hardly refrain from smiling at her petulance. The young woman had for the moment dissolved into the lass. Robert thought of Edward roaming freely through the Crichton forests and moors. Poor lad. Little did he know what tempests awaited him.

"It's your father's reason." Robert spoke more gently this time. Even as he said these things, the words sounded hollow to him. He liked and admired her father, Alexander, very much. Here was a man who had succeeded in filing away many of the burrs of his mercantile world by bringing culture and learning to his family. But there were some burrs that resisted filing. He would have been horrified to find that the learning he had fostered in his daughter to make a good wife for the husband he chose for her had given her the mind to make that choice for herself.

"And is that your consolation for me?"

Robert could not answer.

"Does not your own heart speak differently?"

This time he blushed. His heart was speaking volumes to him and all at variance to what his tongue had just said. By this point Isabel had taken his hand into her own and kissed it. "It's you I love, Robert. Please take me away from all this. Please."

Although Isabel was hardly a Potiphar's wife, Robert knew he should have taken Joseph's course and left at that moment. It would have been the kinder thing to do. But his own affection for Isabel overmastered him for the moment, and in that time he lingered just long enough to offer Isabel a glimmer of hope.

"Then you love me, too?"

Robert withdrew his hand from hers. "I cannot."

Isabel needed to say nothing. Her reproachful look echoed all the words he had spoken about the will. She wiped away her tears. At once she became his student again and reached for one of his books.

"Ah, *De officiis*. 'On duty.' Since you have, it seems, learned yours, perhaps I shall learn mine." Her voice chilled him. The next hour was the longest he had ever spent.

"You'll not be staying, Rob Henryson," Father Ninian said when Robert went to see him for confession after the Inglis family returned to Edinburgh. Ninian, the parish priest at St. Margaret's in the Cowgate, was a wee wiry man, with a face that looked like the cracked sole of a shoe left days in the rain and sun. That's because he had spent his youth in the campaigns of James II. But he had been exposed to more than rain and sun. The exploding cannon that had killed James at the siege of Roxburgh Castle had singed forever the hair from Ninian's face. It had also singed from him the love of his riotous life (for which he had been notorious) and had ignited in him a charity (for which he was now famous). His was a charity like a coulter in a blacksmith's forge. Glowing red, but iron nonetheless. He knew from experience the vagaries of the human heart and wished to spare his penitents the dreams that still plagued his sleep.

"You'll be leaving," the old man continued, "before the crack in your heart widens to a chasm. Once that happens, there'll be no jumping back over it."

"You'll be shriving away my livelihood." The protest sounded lame, even to Robert's own ears.

"Your mother's remarried and your sibs are all grown. You've lived as a poor scholar once. It'll not harm you to live that way again. More to the point, I'll not have you being an Abelard to Sandie Inglis' Heloise. Besides, he's destined her for one greater than a poor schoolmaster like yourself." Father Ninian's absolutions brooked no debate, and he ended the confession abruptly with a benediction.

That evening Robert gave notice to Alexander Inglis and within the month he was gone. He left behind one who under his tutelage had cultivated a fair hand for letters, a fine ear for poetry, and a nimble mind for sums. He took with him a wistful heart and a quarto of Chaucer's Troilus. The unsuspecting Alexander had commissioned it from a notary and scribe who handled most of his legal documents. Although the manuscript was by no means a *deluxe* edition, it had cost the merchant dearly; but such was his thanks that now his sons could enter the world of trade with greater confidence and his daughter was all the more marriageable for the learning that cast a patina on her more obvious charms. Robert heard nothing further from the family for over twenty years.

He returned to Glasgow to salve his heart's ache with the most effective medicine he knew, his studies. In the stark light of the university, away from the distractions of Edinburgh, he realized the snare he had barely escaped and now understood the wisdom of Father Ninian's counsel—command really. Why should the foolish attraction to a wee slip of a lass mar his satisfaction with God's good gift? This he reminded himself of an evening when he lay awake in his chamber, even while pictures of Isabel flashed before his restless mind.

Within two years, Robert earned a licentiate in canon and civil laws. Another three years and he became a notary—public, imperial, and apostolic—able to validate all legal transactions, both sacred and secular. A comfortable career, either oiling the wheels of Scottish justice or teaching others to do so, seemed assured. Still, the son could not forget the haggard and despondent face of the father who issued from the archdeacon's consistory court, nor did he ever lose that young boy's sense of fairness.

There were, he discovered, other alternatives, some positively good, that poor men like Joshua Henryson might come to envision for their sons. One might use the law to extricate those innocents caught in its viscous web, whose righteous causes might give the Church a case of spiritual indigestion.

That's how it should have been, but perhaps Robert's father knew something he didn't. If David and the other prophets, inspired by the Holy Spirit, had so little effect on the chosen people of God, what change could he hope to work in these dark times among these dark minds? Within ten years he was sitting before Henry Crichton, abbot of the Benedictine convent in Dunfermline. The grammar school needed a new master.

❖

Sleep was an impossibility now. A fable had been forming itself all this while in his head and now demanded to be released. He arose and re-lit the candle. The scratching under his bed began even before he put pen to parchment. He wrote the story of a man like his father, caught between two predators, a wolf who claimed the oxen unjustly, and a fox who might see some justice done, but only at a price. When confronted by the wolf, to whom he had promised the unruly oxen in a fit of anger, the plowman argued:

> "a man may say in grief,
> And then gainsay, if he reflect and see.
> I swear to steal, am I therefore a thief?
> God forbid, sir, all oaths upheld should be.
> Gave I my hand or obliging," said he,
> "Or have ye witness or writ for to show?
> Sir, reive me not, but go and seek the law."

Such appeals, the plowman continued, have no effect on the earth. A lord's word is as "certain as his seal." Besides, as the proverb says, "Without faith all other virtues are not worth a flea." The wolf was adamant that a man's word is his bond, so both parties agreed to let the fox act as a "judge amicable" and swore to abide by his sentence.

The fox went to work immediately, first taking the plowman aside:

> "Friend, thou art in blunder brought;

The wolf will not forgive thee an ox hide.
Yet would myself fain help thee, if I might,
But I am loath to hurt my conscience aught.
Lose not thy quarrel in thy own defence;
This thrives only at great cost and expence.

"See you not that bribes grease cases through,
And gifts cause crooked matters hold full even?
A hen gratefully given saves a cow.
All are not holy that heave their hands to heaven."

When the plowman agreed to the lesser sacrifice, the fox then turned
to the wolf, offering him, in compensation for the loss of the oxen, a huge
cheese lying at the bottom of a well. The wolf eagerly agreed to

"quit-claim the man of all the rest:
His team of oxen? They're not worth a flea;
Yon cheese is meat enough for likes of me."

The wolf demanded that the fox get in a bucket to retrieve the cheese.
Then, when the fox protested that the cheese is so large he cannot handle
it by himself, the wolf greedily climbed in the bucket at the other end of
the rope. On his way down, his weight drew the fox up.

Then angrily the wolf upon him cries:
"I come thus down, why dost thou upward rise?"
"Sir," said the fox, "thus fares it of fortune:
As one comes up, she wheels another down."

Robert smiled grimly. Joshua Henryson would gladly have paid a hen to
see the wolfish abbot of Kelso descending in Fortune's well bucket.

IV

The Cock and the Jewel

Because of his restless night, Robert slept well past the morning meal. Father Charles came to check on him, bringing with him a bowl of broth and a mug of ale. Robert attempted to rise, but the effort was too great.

"Stay, my friend." Charles handed him the bowl and mug. Robert sipped the steaming broth, while Charles went to draw up a stool. Noticing the manuscript on the writing desk, Charles read, "'The Fables of Aesop the Phrygian.' So this is how you spend your evenings." He snorted in mock contempt. "Ever the schoolmaster."

"And what would you have me write?"

"Something more scurrilous, perhaps? Like your Chaucer. At least your confessions would be a wee bit more interesting."

"I'm sorry ever to have taught you to read. Did you not know that he begged pardon for most of his verse?"

"Nay, I am not that far yet. You taught me to read, but I'm still that slow."

"Slow indeed. It's the Reeve's and the Miller's tales—the bawdy ones— you'll have fixed your eyes on, and you'll not read further."

Charles grinned.

"You'd do well to read the first of *my* tales."

"The Cock and the Jewel?"

"Aye, that's the one."

24

Charles began to read aloud.

> A cock there was, with feathers fresh and gay,
> Lively and proud, albeit he was poor,
> Flew forth upon a dunghill soon by day;
> To get his dinner only was his care.
> Scraping among the ash, a jewel fair
> Besmudged he found—beautiful, right precious—
> Was cast forth in sweeping of the house.
>
> So marveling upon the stone, said he,
> "O gentle jewel, O rich and noble thing,
> Though I thee find, I nothing gain from thee;
> Thou art a jewel for a lord or king.
> Pity it were thou should in this midden
> Be buried thus among this muck and mold,
> And thou so fair and worth so mickle gold.
>
> "I love far better things of less avail,
> Like dregs or corn, my empty womb to fill."

Charles stopped reading and patted his stomach for effect. "I can hardly blame the cock. A body cannot eat jewels."

"Aye." Robert shook his head sadly. "That's the damnable thing. Still," he added, with a wan smile, "it would make for a hard turd. These days I'd give anything for one of those." He handed Charles the half-full bowl. "I can eat no more. The ale I'll keep by my bedside."

"I'll check on you later, then. Rest yourself some more." Charles took the bowl and left.

Robert settled back on his pillow and thought back to the time when he had introduced himself to the schoolboys at Dunfermline. From the start he made it clear what the value of their learning was. For the occasion he had written the fable of the cock and the jewel and had attached to it this *moralitas*:

> Who may be hardy, rich, and gracious?
> Who can eschew peril and chance ventures?
> Who can govern a realm, city, or house
> Without knowledge? No man, I you assure.

It is riches that ever shall endure,
Which moth, nor mold, nor other rust can fret:
To all men's souls it is eternal meat.

He had also made it clear to them his feelings on the current state of learning:

Bot now, alas, this jewel is lost and hid.
We seek it not, nor prize it for to find.

Abbot Henry Crichton, during his interview of Robert, had made a similar point about conditions at the abbey school.

Brother Luke, the guestmaster, had ushered the candidate into an office located on the second story of the abbot's residence, built at the northeast end of the abbey precinct. From the front window, the abbot could observe the lives of his fellow monks; from a back window facing the high street, the heart of the burgh. In both of these worlds he had a vital stake.

Although brief, Robert's experience in the law had trained him to observe the slightest nuances in the word and movement of others. Throughout their conversation, Abbot Henry leaned forward in his chair, his elbows on his knees, his hands clasped tightly, as if in fierce prayer. His face was a study in contrasts. The youthful skin of his forehead was folded in perpetual worry. His lips seldom relaxed into a smile, but often remained grimly pressed together. Only when released to allow words to pass did they betray a surprising sensuality, which suggested that the intensity of his gaze might turn just as easily to things of the flesh as to matters of the spirit. To Robert's mind, the abbot was a man struggling to achieve mastery of himself as well as of his abbey.

How difficult Henry's mastery of himself had been, only he and God knew. Robert and most of Scotland were familiar with his difficulties as to subduing the abbey. A member of the powerful Crichton clan, Henry had come to his position as Abbot of Dunfermline by virtue of his family connections. He was already the Abbot of Paisley and Dunfermline was yet a higher rung on the ecclesiastical ladder. The appointment did not come without struggle, however. Alexander Thomson, a member of the abbey, had been elected by his fellow monks, but the pope had overridden the election in deference to the king's choice. Although Thompson did not pursue the matter—ecclesiastical and royal power was stacked overwhelmingly against him—his fellow monks were outraged. An account of the proceedings circulated throughout the monastic houses in the kingdom:

> The abbacy of Dunfermline vacant, the convent chose one of their own monks, called Alexander Thomson; and the King promoted Henry Crichton, abbot of Paisley, thereto, who was preferred by the Pope, through the King's supplications, to the said abbacy. And so then first began such manner of promotion of seculars to abbacies by the King's supplications; and the godly erections were frustrated and decayed because that the Court of Rome admitted the prince's supplications, the rather that they got great profit and sums of money thereby; wherefore the bishops dared not confirm them that were chosen by the convent; nor they who were elected dared not pursue their own right. And so the abbeys came to secular abuses, the abbots and priors being promoted forth of the court who lived court-like, secularly and voluptuously. And then ceased all religious and godly minds and deeds.

This account, which was supposed to be secret, came to Henry's attention; and though he never found the author, he had on his lap all he could handle in establishing his authority.

"The boys are wanting discipline." The abbot was concluding the interview and spoke with some agitation. He stood and turned his back to Robert, resting his hands on the stone sill of the window overlooking the abbey grounds. The expanse of green between his house and chapel, then to the dormitory beyond, was slowly filling up with the graves of the brothers who had completed their mortal tasks.

"Master Cuthbert, God rest him, grew lax in his old age." Henry turned around. "You have little time left to redeem the older boys. They have the means to distinguish themselves, but few have the will. Have you will enough for them?"

These words only confirmed Robert's ruminations about mastery. He sensed in the abbot's request a mixture of motives. A genuine concern for the welfare of the boys' spiritual and intellectual life, tainted with jealousy for his abbey's reputation perhaps? Promises of distinction in the boys meant little if they did not achieve distinction. Unfulfilled promises made the failure only more pronounced.

"Aye, my lord abbot. I have the will."

"Good. Scotland is in dark days. Her king is but twenty-two, not long past his minority. The need for men of character to help him guide the realm grows increasingly desperate. The vultures feasted on the carcass of James II's reign, and I fear there is little left for the young James to rule well."

The exploding cannon, which had killed a king and scarred Father Ninian, had left Scotland once again in the fragile fingers of a boy heir, subject to the inevitable maneuvering, whether subtle or spectacular, for power. Pushed to one side or trampled underfoot was justice—the one virtue Robert had unsuccessfully represented as advocate. The faces of those he had failed gathered before his mind's eye, and on the lips of each was that one word: "justice." It was before these witnesses still assembled in his imagination that he spoke: "Few desires are stronger in me than peace and order in the kingdom, my lord abbot."

"The position is yours. Brother Luke will show you about the grounds and settle you in your quarters."

"Thank you, my lord."

"*Pax vobiscum.*" The abbot signed the blessing of the cross and rang a bell. Brother Luke appeared almost immediately, as if he had been waiting behind the door for just such a signal.

"You will find the brothers here most agreeable," the guestmaster said, as he and Robert crossed the grounds from the abbot's house to the church. There, using his finger as a pointer, Luke traced the Scoto-Norman stonework with its geometric designs and reverently paused by the tombs of Robert the Bruce and his family and of the shrine to St. Margaret. From there, they walked through the cloisters to the refectory, whose southern wall sprang out of the hillside to form a massive man-made cliff four stories high. The large windows set in this wall here gave a commanding view of the abbey's granges. Luke paused for a time before one of the windows, as if soaking up as much of the vision and the warmth as he could. He was chosen well for his task. He lingered at each point, as if he, too, were seeing the abbey for the first time.

Luke shook off his reverie. "The library and scriptorium are one flight below us. They are the demesne of Brother Dominic." The two descended by the narrow stone turret. "There are fifteen hundred manuscripts," he added proudly. By Scottish standards the collection was enormous.

"Your classroom is here," Luke said of the room yet another flight of stairs below the library. Though not as large or imposing as those in the refectory, the windows here still caught the southern sun, giving maximum light for the winter hours. No fire burned in the huge fireplace to take off the northern chill, even this late in the summer, since the students would not be returning until the Michaelmas term.

28

As they began to descend one more flight of stairs, they met Father Charles, the cellarer, ascending after his weekly inventory of the wines and ales. He was a heavy-set man, one who took a personal interest in the quality of his food and drink. Luke and Robert began to back up the narrow turret, but he waved them to follow him down. He obviously welcomed the opportunity to show Luke's guest the cellar himself.

After the introductions, he drew off two half tankards of ale from the nearest cask and passed one to Robert. When Luke declined the other, he began to drink from it himself.

"That's very fine." Robert nodded in genuine approval.

"Do you think so?"

"Aye, indeed."

Charles grinned broadly. "It's not bad, is it? We have our own brewery, which I oversee. In a former life I was a brewer. Finish that off and I'll draw you one of the darker ales." He led them to another tun and, after garnering Robert's praise for that variety, led them to yet another. He was about to introduce Robert to the wines, which he had imported—"at great savings to the abbey," he confessed—from Spain, Portugal, France, and Italy, but Luke took Robert's arm.

"I must get Master Robert settled in his lodgings, Father Charles. And no doubt you have a full morning yourself."

"Aye, laddie." The teeth flashed again. Charles took Robert by the hand. "Another time, then." With no more effect than if he had drunk water, the cellarer led the other two up the stairs. Luke followed Robert, on whom the drink had more dire consequences.

Luke ushered his guest through the dormitory to his cell. "I will show you the abbot's great hall later"—he paused meaningfully—"when conditions are more suitable." As a lay member of the abbey, Robert was given a private room to which was attached a small oratory for reflection and writing. "I trust you will find your quarters satisfactory." Luke smiled as Robert sat down on his bed. "You'll have to forgive Father Charles. He forgets that others do not have his, uhm, capacities. The only effect the ale ever seems to have on him is to increase his girth."

"He alluded to a former life." Robert spoke with great deliberation so as not to slur his words.

"Aye. It's a tragic tale, true enough, but one all too common. He was indeed a brewer just outside Galashiels. While he was away in Edinburgh, reivers burned his home and brewery. The shock drove his wife to deliver their unborn child early. Neither mother nor bairn lived. When Charles sought to become a brother, the former abbot, Richard de Bothwell, God rest his soul, sought to dissuade him: 'To run from pain is not to run to God.'

"But Charles was that persistent. 'I'm not certain but pain is God's own herd dog running me to ground,' he told Abbot Richard. He even became a priest, though he half mangles the Latin of Mother Church. More like a butcher, he is." Luke pulled at his ear. "Still, it was one of my lord abbot's wisest decisions. I'll leave you to yourself for now. If I can be of further assistance—"

Robert nodded gratefully, trying to stifle a yawn.

Luke bowed and left. Robert lay down. After a moment, he heard the bell calling the brothers to sext. He fell asleep to the chant of Psalm 118. The last thing he heard was "*Super omnes docentes me intellexi quia testimonia tua meditatio mea est.*" "I have understood more than all my teachers," Robert murmured to himself and smiled.

Fumey visions of Charles, Isabel, and Brother Luke moved about absurdly in his dreams under the stern eye of Abbot Crichton. He slept through the midday meal.

That evening, Father Charles drew up next to Robert after vespers on their way to the dormitory. "Brother Luke chided me for being too hospitable this morning." The grin was unrepentant.

"It was, shall I say, both potent and profuse. Both were welcome, though."

Charles then said something strange, as if he could read Robert's heart, but would not address the matter directly. "Leaving something—or someone—dear will be the way of most brothers here. Perhaps it's been taken from them or maybe they've given it up on their own. In either case, there's no real leaving, not if it was really dear to begin with. The gift that's been pressed into the hand leaves a scar, even when the gift itself has long since gone." Charles had never taken his eyes off Robert, but now they seemed to look through him, as if into another world. He was no longer smiling. "I'm thinking that it's the way of all gifts. They would not be a gift otherwise."

With only a wink as an explanation, Charles padded off to his cell. Robert wondered at these words and found himself looking at his palms, half expecting to see scars.

Several days later, the abbot called Robert into his office. "Are you finding your accommodations adequate?"

"Aye, quite comfortable."

"Good." Only the flicker of a smile and then the lips pressed together.

"It is my custom to assign a confessor to each member of the community, whether lay or clergy. Father Charles shall be yours."

"As you wish, my lord abbot."

"As God wishes," Abbot Crichton replied and added, "and Father Charles." For the first time, the abbot came close to an actual laugh.

Robert left, shaking his head at the thought of his laying bare his heart to a brewer turned priest, whose learning extended no further than the Latin required to recite the Mass and read Holy Writ. As all that was haughty and proud in him rose to object, he remembered Charles' words from the earlier night. Robert was then conscious of a burning in his hands. He realized that he had clinched them into a fist. Opening them and raising the palms to his face, he cried, for the first time in a great while.

The following month, Robert devoted much time to preparing his lessons. He reacquainted himself with his Aristotle, Cicero, Lucan, and Virgil. The boys in his care would require a stringent grounding in the trivium—their grammar, rhetoric, and logic—if they were to go to university or enter the civil service.

At the same time, he did not neglect his poetry. He read and re-read Chaucer's Troilus book that Alexander Inglis had given him. Although lacking the range one might find in the tales of Canterbury, the Troilus was marked by an unrelenting honesty that would not allow the characters, however attractive or sympathetic they might be, to escape the consequences of their choices.

One day, after coming to the end of the book for yet another time, Robert walked about the abbey grounds to rest his eyes. Barely conscious of where he was going, he ended up in the cellar, where he found Father Charles making his inventory.

"A sample of our latest?" Charles asked, reaching for a tankard.

Robert waved his hand, but Charles insisted. "No more than one. At the most, six, I promise." He pulled a draft for Robert and himself from the nearest tun. "What brings you to a place so far out of your way, besides the desire to extort from me an illicit dram?" He took a swig and lowered the tankard. A great red tongue swept his upper lip to remove the foam dripping from his mustache. He shoved a stool in Robert's direction and took one for himself. "Unless it's to make confession, in which case I pronounce this penance: For each gill of ale you've drunk, you must piss as much again. You'll not be keeping your ill-gotten gains." Charles raised his tankard in salute.

"It's not so serious as all that," Robert laughed and met Charles' tankard with his own.

"A prelude like that and I usually suspect the worst."

"Nay, I just been reading and sought some company in the interval."

"Reading?"

"Aye. Chaucer."

"Chaucer, eh?" Charles shook his head. "I am no literary man. I can rhyme numbers to meet my purpose and my accounts are neat, but it's spoken stories my mother would be telling me, tales of ordinary folk. Stories learned and fine never made their way into our poor cottage. But you'll tell me, will you?" Charles pulled another draft and listened intently as Robert recited the rise and fall of the great Trojan affair between Troilus and Cresseid: their love-sickness, their consummation, their separation, and Cresseid's betrayal with the Greek hero Diomede.

"I've done little justice to my master, but there you have it," Robert concluded.

"A sad tale and no mistake," Charles said, shaking his head. "My old mother would have liked that one. What happened to Cresseid?"

"Chaucer never tells. She betrayed once. Perhaps, like the beautiful Helen of Troy, she betrayed again."

"Or she was betrayed. Your Chaucer's Diomede seems unlikely to keep troth once he had his way with a woman. It would not be hard to imagine a desperate Cresseid passing from one man to another. Mightn't your Cresseid be driven to seek shelter where she could?" Charles sighed. "All that beauty gone to waste."

"Aye," Robert said quietly. "All that beauty gone to waste."

"Well, Cook will be wondering what's been keeping me."

"I doubt he'll be wondering too hard." Robert laughed.

Charles pulled from his pouch a sprig of licorice and began to chew it. "To hide the evidence." He winked.

Robert, who was still not ready to go back to his writing, meandered through the great gateway, known as the pend, that led from the abbey precinct down to the lower part of the burgh and further on to the farmlands that composed only a small portion of the abbey's rich holdings. The sun, which over the dying weeks of summer cast longer and longer shadows ever earlier set the barley fields alight. Before too many days the tenants would be harvesting the crop; and when the fields turned to stubble, the boys would return.

The sound of several clappers interrupted these thoughts. A small band of lepers had reached the outskirts of the burgh, presumably on their trek to the leper hospital in Stirling.

"Alms," they cried when they saw him. He dropped several pennies into the outstretched pouches and shuddered at the misery of these folk. During the evening meal, which the brothers ate in silence, the lector read from the story of the Syrian commander Naaman, who was healed of his leprosy by Elijah. Afterwards, Robert returned to his cell. For a time, he sat at his writing desk, his forehead resting on clenched fists, a single piece of parchment at his elbows. He straightened suddenly and repeated once again, "All that beauty gone to waste." He then began to write.

V

The Wolf and the Wether

Charles came in later that afternoon to bring yet another bowl of broth. Robert turned his head.

"I know." Charles was apologetic. "But Cook fears you'll not be able to hold down a solid piece of beef."

"Hold it down, hold it in—it's all one. I can do neither," Robert replied. "Still, in a short time, it will make little difference." He saw his friend's distressed look and changed the subject. "Will you read to me?"

Robert knew that he asked of his friend a costly gift. Even after all these years, reading aloud was still painful business to this man who could better judge the character of a wine than a text. But Robert was restless and desired the company.

"If I must read, it'll be another of your fables." Charles had a childlike taste for stories. Robert nodded.

"The Tale of the Wolf and the Wether," Charles began. He read of the death of a faithful old sheepdog and the shepherd's great fear that he would lose his defenseless flock to the wolves and would then have to beg for food and "with pikestaff and with pouch to fare in town."

The ram of the flock, the bell-wether, overheard the shepherd's moan and devised a plan.

"Master," said he, "make merry and be blythe:

34

To break your heart for sorrow is not right;
For one dead dog ye should not pine away.
Go fetch him now and fast his skin off flay;
Then sew it on me—and look that it be neat,
Both head and neck, body, tail, and feet.

"Then will the wolf believe that I am he,
If he pursues, by God, I shall not spare
To follow him as fast as did your hound.
I warrant that of sheep ye'll not lose one pound."

So successful was the ram in his disguise that no predator came near the flock. That is, until a wolf, close to starvation, took the risk and stole a lamb. As before, the ram gave chase, but emboldened by his previous good fortune, he pressed his advantage, crying out that it was not the lamb, but the wolf himself he wanted. Throughout the countryside they ran. Only after they tore their way through some briars did the wolf notice a strange thing:

He saw the wether come crashing through the briars,
Then saw the dog's skin hanging on his flanks.
"Nay," said he, "is this ye, that is so near?
Right now a hound, and now white as a friar?

"Thrice, by my soul, ye caused me shit behind:
Upon my haunch the signs it may be seen;
For terror full oft I defiled the wind."

Despite the ram's protests that he followed only in sport, the wolf was too angry after his fright to forgive and forget. The tattered dog's skin offered little protection against sharp fangs.

Charles, who was much more interested in the story than in the accompanying morals, made to put the manuscript aside.

"You've not read the *moralitas*," Robert objected. "Go on."

Charles reluctantly took up the manuscript again.

Here may thou see that riches of array
Will cause poor men presumptuous for to be;
They think they owe to none, be they as gay,

But counterfeit a lord in all degree.
Out of their case in pride they climb so high
That they forbear their betters in no stead,
Until some man tips their heels over their head.

It was Charles' turn to object. "This conclusion ill suits the fable."

Robert smiled at the intensity of his friend's tone. "You think not?"

"It fits as poorly as the dog's skin on the sheep."

"In what way?"

"The sheep did all in his power to protect his fellows. How could he be accused of presumption?"

"Some are ill-suited to tasks that lie before them."

Something began to dawn on Charles. "And is that why you left the practicing of the law?"

Robert had not meant for the conversation to go in that direction. The decision to return to teaching had been made before he had ever met Charles. It was a topic he could avoid with his friend because he still performed legal duties for the abbey. No one could question his motives. Others must certainly conclude that teaching had only given him greater scope. He could not avoid the direct question—Charles knew him too well. Nor did he want to avoid the question. Not now. Not so close to the end of his life.

Robert sought for a way to begin. "The law turned out to be a galled nag that limps along under the weight of a fat master. She sometimes gets where she's meant to be, but not before the master has supped and drunk at every inn along the way."

"A pretty piece of poetry. Now what does it mean?"

"It was not the right that always won. And when it did, it seldom won in the right way. Cunning was of more value than learning, though learning could feed cunning. Justice had but a piping wee voice in a chamber filled with the girning of wolves. In that university were many masters, though the one I was apprenticed to was among the best. William Cunningham, he was. Behind his back his fellows called him 'Wiley.' More of a fox he seemed—lean, almost gaunt, with russet hair was so thick, his bonnet would spring about on his head as he paced about the chamber."

"A very Reynard." Charles laughed.

"Aye, and that's not all. His nose and ears were forested with stiff red bristles."

"And good at his profession?"

"Indeed. Much sought after, he was, even by poor litigants, and he undertook most suits: the rich on the poor, the poor on the rich, the rich on the rich. In all he stood to gain somehow, through handsome settlements or recoveries. It's the way of law that one party always loses. The cunning Master Cunningham always won. One type of suit he never undertook, however."

"The poor on the poor?"

"Aye. That he called a Lenten feast."

"But did he not care for justice at all?"

"That's the curious thing. He did care, in his own fashion. In cases of manifest injustice, he would arrange settlements (at some benefit to himself, to be sure). In that way, neither party won or lost over greatly. 'I've my scruples, laddie,' he would tell me."

Robert paused. The memories of this part of his life were a painful mixture. He loathed the careless ease with which the lawyers could dismiss from their minds the human misery of their trade so soon after the suits had passed. Burgh courts and justice ayres were celebrations for the local folk who, in addition to buying and selling wares and to swapping gossip, watched opposing advocates wield the sword of law in legal jousts. With even greater eagerness crowds gathered to witness the results that often ensued from such battles—the maiming or hanging of some notorious felon.

The lawyers were only too aware of their roles and often played them with all the energy of the villainous Pharoah or Herod from the mystery plays. In the better of the lawyers, such enthusiasm only sharpened their faculties; and if they preened themselves like so many vain Chauntecleers, they also fought with the fury of cockerels in the pit. Afterwards, in the King's Arms or Stag's Head or Lion and Thistle or other such local tavern, advocates and prosecutors, fierce adversaries just hours before, would raise a tankard and regale one another to stories of past combats and past mentors, now grown to the stuff of legend.

Robert raised his tankard with the others, but the nearby gibbet, where swung a body not yet cold, cast a long, lingering shadow on his imagination. Many, perhaps most, of those who hung out there deserved their fate, guilty of some violence. But how many had turned to theft, hoping, if caught, to find the court's mercy by appealing to that fundamental maxim, "Need has no law"? How many peasant folk were even now making their way home in a world darkened by evening and despair?

All the rhetorical figures of shorn sheep and rapacious wolves—from Scripture and from the rantings of radical priests like William Langland—

were not the less true because they were well worn. As a lad, Robert had seen carcasses of sheep that had wandered too far from the flock. He had even come across the mangled body of one that yet had life, its torn belly heaving, its eyes rolling about in anguish. He had slit its throat to extinguish its misery. Few in this room filled with peat smoke, ale, and laughter would have known the smell or feel of reeking blood or the devastating effect the loss of even one animal had on a family whose survival could be measured in bawbees and pence rather than shillings and pounds. Or so he suspected.

These memories contested with others—those of Master William—that were not entirely unpleasant. Although horrified at first and uncomfortable throughout by the old man's practical turn of mind, he could not help but marvel at Cunningham's ability to maneuver the evidence like so many chess pieces until the jury had no choice but to declare, "Checkmate." Besides this, he was an excellent companion—charming, urbane, equally conversant in the political philosophy of Marsilius of Padua or the poetry of James I or the Code of Justinian and the Decretals of Gratian. He also had the uncanny ability to create in apprentices like young Robert the illusion that they were his intimates and peers, though a moment's reflection told them how little he ever truly revealed. The intimacy was all one way.

Robert occasionally presumed upon this deceptive frankness to ask Cunningham about the conflicts he felt between law and right, even right and faith. The older man never took offense, although he must have known that such inquiries implicitly criticized his own behavior. Nor did he offer the vague and smiling dismissals of a father to a young child.

"In these dark times we must be wise, Robbie, as our Lord admonishes us, *'ecce ego mitto vos sicut oves in medio luporum estote ergo prudentes sicut serpentes et simplices sicut columbae.'*"

Robert was silent.

"Do you not see the truth in this saying?"

"Aye, I do, but sometimes it seems that we spend an over great time studying to be serpents."

"I grant you, the doves grow scarce and the number of wolves only increases." He paused. "But I'm thinking that your question runs much deeper. You're wondering if we are of the wolf's party, *lupus legis*, neither a serpent nor a dove." William's laughter was disarming. How could Robert despise someone so transparent and at ease with himself? He half expected William to follow with some regretful comment that such things must be in the world of old men, as if to let Robert in on a secret intimate to the legal guild alone. The lawyer said nothing of the kind.

"I'll not be denying that the law has taken on a wolfish cast. We would be forever arguing about which trial found or lost justice. My lord the abbot of Kelso little thought he wronged your father by taxing him." Robert started at the mention of the case. "O aye, I was the abbot's advocate and slept no less soundly when the matter was settled. Your father's plight was grim, but by our law the abbot had the right to tax and your father the duty to pay. I advised the abbot to forgive your father the obligation. He set aside my counsel. How else, he argued, might he escape a like plea from every other tenant on abbey lands? It was then my duty to win his case. I could only pray that afterwards he or someone would show mercy to your father and his family."

It occurred to Robert that someone had. The abbot, a hard man, had been persuaded to accept Robert into the grammar school. Might William have had something to do with that? The old man remained impassive, though. Robert had seen that look often enough in burgh court. It was William's greatest advantage—never to signal his emotions and thus allow an opponent or witness to adapt.

"Would you have the course of your life altered? You can, I'm thinking, give all this over and take up your father's old tack." Robert said nothing and William smiled with his accustomed cunning. "Before much longer you'll have your own wolf skin." When Robert winced, the old man waved his hand as if brushing away an annoying insect. "Or dog's skin, if that image would suit you more. Then you can champion the poor all you wish. But by the law, Robbie. Never forget. Always by the law."

"And did you?" Charles posed the question during a lull in Robert's narrative.

"Champion the poor?"

"Nay, take on the wolf's skin?"

"I studied, my friend, harder than ever I had at university, so as to learn the ways of the sheepdog and not a wolf."

"Which did you become?"

Robert could tell that Charles found the story amusing and that he already suspected the answer. He blushed. "Neither."

"Neither?"

"Aye. I have not the wit to learn either way. Underneath, I'm a sheep and ever shall be. I tried to practice the wiles of Master William," Robert continued, "but it's as if my dogskin had ripped. Others saw the tear."

Charles laughed.

"What is it?" Robert asked.

"The picture of you in some mouth-eaten dog's skin, my friend." Charles patted Robert's arm. "Whatever you say, my heart is with the bellwether. After all, he did the work when there was no one else to do it. You show too much grace to men like the abbot of Kelso, who would see any challenge to authority as presumptuous. Were you presumptuous to see justice done?"

Robert knew that Charles had extended him grace and in the mirror of his friend's compassion he could smile with forgiveness at the antic fool he saw there. "Aye, you're in the right. But it was not just that."

"What was it, then?"

"There were other lessons I learned too, hard ones and little to my credit. I allowed myself to be duped by one client into believing that he had an easy suit against the laird George Hamilton, who was notorious for abusing the law to enlarge his estates. It looked so simple—a man of poor means seeking redress from a rich oppressor. Only in this instance, my client was acting on behalf of an even greater vulture—Robert Colquhoun, the Bishop of Argyle."

Charles signed the cross in mock benediction for this blasphemy. "Go on," he urged, smiling.

"O, the trap they laid was elegant, with just enough truth in the claim to convince me to represent the poor man. Had the case succeeded, Hamilton's power would have been seriously weakened. I swallowed the bait like a glutton, more hungry to see Hamilton beaten than justice done in this particular suit. Greed comes in many guises."

"Greed for justice?" Charles asked.

"Can a just end follow from a greedy motive?" Robert was silent for a moment.

"What happened?"

"I stirred up a hornet's nest well and truly. Hamilton unleashed a hound of his own, Gavin Armstrong, to humiliate me."

"Gavin Armstrong?"

"An attorney of great renown and even greater ruthlessness. He was named well. Strong was the arm that manhandled me in the burgh court."

"And your client?"

"He was fined for a false claim. I was fortunate enough to keep him from something more severe. Hamilton was that angry."

"What about the bishop?"

"The old fox was was never exposed. I only pray that he did well by his poor factor."

Robert smiled, but some of the pain still lingered in his memory. "I might as well have carried a leper's cup and clapper with me when I entered the tavern, that's how welcome I was."

"And what happened to your Master Cunningham?"

"He retired with more than enough money to live a comfortable, even fine life, then gave most of it away."

"Gave it away?"

"Aye. He bought a wee cottage outside of Peebles where he spent the rest of his life minding a garden and reading. His neighbors discovered him sitting in a chair by his hearth with a book on his lap." Robert interpreted Charles' silence as a question. "It was Augustine's *Confessions*."

At this point, the abbey bells summoned the brothers to compline.

"Here, then, I've kept you too long," Charles said, rising suddenly. He arranged Robert's blanket and prepared to leave. Robert took his hand. "Perhaps you could bring George and a notary tomorrow. It's long past that I should be making out my last will and testament."

"Aye. That I'll do."

When Charles reached the door, Robert called out, "The poor will be missing Master William, for all his serpent ways."

VI

The Bloody Shirt

After Charles left, Robert lay back, thinking. He envied the others their sleepy devotion and the rise and fall of their chant, like North Sea waves on a Fife pier. After he retired from his teaching, he had frequently attended divine service throughout the day, although this had never been expected of him. He was especially fond of special feast days, when Abbot George authorized the celebration of the sung Mass. On occasions, the choirmaster performed the Mass composed by one of their own, Ingram Bannatyne. Robert had enough training in music to know that the choice was not out of misguided loyalty. Ingram, in his short career, had achieved an enviable mastery.

Ingram. In his twenty some years as schoolmaster, Robert had seldom found a student so difficult to like as Ingram Bannatyne. Great creating Nature had done little to endear Ingram to the eye. It was as if she had withdrawn nearly all her favors and had assembled him from the worst of parents' features: his father's lumbering frame and huge ears; his mother's heavy eyelids, which gave the appearance of perpetual drowsiness, and her coarse auburn hair, which stuck out like straw in all directions. He and his mother had enough hair between them, so the other choristers teased, that his father—a thatcher by trade—might roof an entire cathedral.

Even now Robert could envision the boy plodding lethargically along the abbey hallways, or blinking stupidly at his empty slate, as if an answer would magically appear, or protesting in that high-pitched whine at the taunts of his classmates. As schoolmaster, Robert was bound to admonish the other boys, and he always summoned up enough self-control to do so. Secretly, however, he found it difficult not to side with them.

One gift Nature had bestowed on Ingram greatly outweighed the defects. The boy could sing.

Brother Martin, master of the song school, had recounted to Robert the day when Ingram's parents brought their son for an audition. "Heard him singing while bundling straw," father Bannatyne told Martin. "I've little learning for music; but when I closed my eyes, there I was in the abbey church."

This was no boast of an overly proud father. When Ingram opened his mouth to sing, Brother Martin could hardly contain his joy. So delicate and light was music in the boy's voice that it seemed already fully formed in him and sought simply to be released.

His performance in the grammar school, however, was another matter altogether. He resisted at each step the grammar, rhetoric, and logic that were to be his daily fare. Robert often wondered whether the father had early on given over the struggle to lead this dull, stubborn ox of a boy in directions he refused to go and had entrusted that task to the patience of Mother Church. But then hadn't the blessed Thomas Aquinas been known as the "Dumb Ox"? What might Providence hold in store for this lad? Might he, like St. Thomas, strain at his yoke to pull an age to glory?

As time went on, Robert began to feel sorry for Ingram. Life for the boy seemed to be one cruel joke. Nature's gift later proved a burden. Long after the voices of the other choristers changed, his never deepened one wit, and the hair on his face never grew beyond a soft down. Had he, they asked, lost his cullions to a butcher's knife? Even Fortune conspired against him. An encounter with the apprentices from the burgh had cost him the sight in one eye. The band of the patch that he now wore only accentuated the size of his ears and the unruliness of his hair.

Among his fellows Ingram had only two companions—George Crichton and John de Leith. George, the recognized leader of the choristers, would grin at the teasing of the others, but never joined them. After a time, he persuaded Ingram to join in the mischief he organized. Ingram rewarded this trust with a fierce loyalty. Once, when the choristers were playing the town boys in an illicit game of football, a fight broke out. Although ill equipped by temperament to defend himself properly, Ingram never left George's side and received a concussion and severe bruises for his pains. After that, George accorded him the honor due a hero and took a custodial interest in him, as a lord might a favored minion. All teasing stopped. This rooted only more deeply Ingram's notion of loyalty, and in the winds that were to follow he was to be broken for that loyalty. But these were happier days.

Unlike George, John he bestowed on Ingram equality rather than lordship. They both seemed bound by some great unhappiness, which their friendship lessened. The two boys—one tall, almost skeletal, the other short and fleshy—made a strange pair wandering about the abbey precinct or by the edge of one the granges. Robert, watching from his oratory window the boys deep in conversation, sometimes arm in arm, feared their intimacy, partly because of the temptations to the flesh it posed, but moreso the temptations to the spirit, that they would devour one another in their loneliness and pain. He composed a fable by which he sought to warn them of such dangers. It was the old story of the town mouse, who coaxed her sister from a spare life in the uplands to the ease and plenty of the burgh. The promises of a full belly had their price, as the country mouse learned when Gib the cat interrupted their feasting and grabbed hold of the country mouse.

> From foot to foot he cast her just in fun,
> Sometimes up, sometimes down, as frisky as a lamb.
> Sometimes he let her under straw to run;
> Sometimes he winked, and played with her a game;
> Thus on the mouse inflicted he great pain
> Until at last, through fortune and good luck,
> Between the arras and the wall she ducked.

When the cat gave up pursuit and the danger passed, the upland mouse cried out to her sister:

> "Farewell, sister, thy feast here I defy!
> "Thy banquet fine is mingled all with care;
> Thy goose is good, thy sauce is sour as gall;
> Almighty God keep me from such a feast."
> With that she took her leave and forth did go.

> I cannot tell how afterwards she fared,
> But I heard say she passed to her den

As warm as wool, although it was not great,
And snug; her larder stuffed, full to the brim,
With beans and nuts, peas, rye, and wheat;
When she desired, she had enough to eat
In quiet and ease without any dread.

But Robert's fears were unwarranted. Something else had laid greater claims upon Ingram than fealty to George or love for John. He often withdrew even from these two companions, preferring instead the solitary company of his own voice and Brother Martin's old gittern. It was on one such occasion, while walking through a deserted copse below the abbey one Sunday afternoon, Robert overheard Ingram singing and playing to the stream that ran there and ventured to the place where the boy sat. Instead of putting down his instrument in embarrassment and standing in respect of his master, Ingram looked up with his one good eye, nodded slightly, and continued. It was as if he were singing in the presence of a higher master to whom he owed a greater respect.

The mere sight of the fragile instrument in the huge lap was enough to provoke laughter, as did the beefy hands that threatened to snap a string or to strangle the slender neck. But as Robert listened, he closed his eyes and saw something much different. That same mouth, from which Latin exercises had to be dragged, released of its own accord note after note, freely and delicately. The instrument he wed to his voice as a helpmeet—demure and plain, but firm.

The song was unfamiliar to Robert, a hymn in the Scots tongue meditating on the joys and sufferings of the Blessed Virgin. It was as if something in the heart of the Holy Mother had found its way into Ingram's voice and fingers. In a variation on a local drinking song, she caroused to the announcement of our Lord's conception in her womb; her contorted body moved to a *danse macabre* as her son stumbled through the streets of Jerusalem towards Golgotha; she wept a lament at his feet on the cross; glided down the nave in a grand cathedral of the Lord's own making to receive her crown as Queen of Heaven. Suffering the boy himself knew, certain enough. But he had also caught glimpses of joy—somewhere, somehow.

When the music ceased, Robert stood in awe. Ingram's head remained bowed toward the instrument. "*Laus Deo,*" Robert heard him whisper.

"God be praised indeed," Robert answered. "What is the piece? I do not recognize it."

Ingram then stood. "It's one of my own. I call it 'O Brooding Passion.'"

"'*O Passio Ferens*,' " Robert echoed.

Ingram smiled. "I like the Scots better."

"Aye," Robert acknowledged. The Latin would divorce the world of the spirit from the world Ingram knew.

"I would learn more. Brother Martin has given me the rudiments, and I am grateful. But he can take me no farther. He admits as much."

"You would to go to Edinburgh, then?" Robert had suspected that this announcement would be coming soon. Brother Martin had more than once declared, "The plant'll soon outgrow the pot." Talent such as this would flourish under William Roger, the great English musician whom Edward IV had commended to the Scottish king. Robert's only fear was the torment Ingram might endure. The boys at the abbey school were but playful puppies compared to what he would find at court. Still, why should the boy not be given some scope? He could always return to the less tumultuous life of an abbey choirmaster.

It was not, however, the Scottish court that Ingram dreamed of. "To France," replied.

"France?" Robert stared at him.

"Aye. I wish to study with Guillaume Dufay."

The aging Dufay was preeminent among continental musicians. Ingram had recently heard his music through the talents of Jacques de l'Isle, one of the French master's pupils. De l'Isle accompanied a French emissary, sent on a hurried visit to Scotland to stitch up a tear in the Auld Alliance. After the cloth was whole again, the negotiators adjourned to the abbot's guest hall, where they dined and were entertained by the boy choristers directed in one of Dufay's recent masses, *Missa l'homme armé*. Robert admired Brother Martin's talents, and would set the choristers of the abbey school against the cathedral choirs of Glasgow or even St. Andrews. There was, however, no doubting the superior musicianship of this Frenchman, nor the extraordinary power of the music. Gentle Brother Martin. He was the first to praise de l'Isle's gifts and also sought out the musician's instruction during the short time he was in Dunfermline.

"Then why shouldn't Ingram go to France?" Robert argued with himself. "Scotland sent her sons abroad to the Europe's finest universities: Paris, Louvain, Leiden, Cologne, Bologna. Why shouldn't one of those sons be his and Brother Martin's?"

"Master Guillaume will little tolerate slovenly effort."

"He'll have no cause."

"And I had cause?"

"Aye, cause enough. But begging your pardon, Master Robert. Words alone cannot fly. It's music that'll give them wing."

Robert spoke to Martin that evening. Ingram had already made his desires known to his choirmaster. "It's a French meadow he'll be wanting"—Martin attempted to console himself— "warmed by a French sun, not some Scottish moor blown about by North Sea sleet." Brother Martin wrote to Jacques de l'Isle and gained an introduction to the celebrated Dufay.

The plan wanted only approval from the lad's parents. This they gave with no hesitation, although they knew that they would be crushed by the debt. Martin, with Robert's voice, convinced the abbot to provide an allowance, with the understanding the Ingram would return to the abbey after a period of three years so as to aid Brother Martin.

The date of Ingram's departure was set for the first of August, three months hence. In that time, Robert undertook to prepare the boy for what lay before him. He set Ingram to study French through texts like the *Roman de Renard* and the various fable collections of Isopet, but prayed that these might also fortify the boy's vulnerable spirit.

One morning, in the middle of their lessons, Ingram asked, "Is it a large country, France?"

Robert laughed. "Aye. She'd swallow wee Scotland three or four times over."

"So you've been there?"

"I accompanied the Bishop of Glasgow to meet a papal delegate at Paris."

"Would you return?"

What to tell the boy? Others might thrive as citizens of the world; but what they called urbane, he found loud and garish, an excuse for licentiousness under the guise of refinement. No, his books were world enough to travel in, the hearts of his fellows numerous enough to explore, the mysteries of God deep enough to plumb. "Some day, perhaps," he added with little enthusiasm.

Robert could feel the intensity of Ingram's gaze and sought to calm his anxiety. "Paris was too large for my taste. I've no doubt Cambrai, where Master Dufay dwells, will be different. Besides, it's few who'll have the gift you do. And it was that gift speaking through you when you first determined to go to France. God'll be stirring our hearts even before we know to ask, and where he stirs, there he'll be. But—" something was stirring him to add— "but it's a gift. Hold too fast to it and you'll strangle it. Strangle it, and it will not stir at all."

Ingram nodded and grew silent. Robert sensed that this was a proper moment to leave. He patted Ingram's arm. "I'm certain that Cambrai will be a most suitable place. Master Dufay, who's been to Italy, would not return there in his old age otherwise."

Robert had hardly left the room when he heard Ingram begin to pluck his gittern, as if translating his thought into notes. He murmured a benediction on the boy.

August came, and ready or not, Ingram took his leave. He was to travel with Brother Martin to Edinburgh, where he could set sail for the Low Countries, then travel south to Cambrai. There was little fanfare at his going. Besides father and mother Bannatyne, the only persons to gather at the pend in the early hours of that Monday morning were the abbot, Robert, Charles, and friends, John and George. Ingram bid a polite and formal farewell to the adults and would have done the same to George, had not the latter brushed the outstretched hand aside.

"I'll not be giving you so stiff a send-off, my faithful comrade-in-arms," George said and laid his hands on both Ingram's shoulders and set his forehead next to Ingram's own. "I'll see you hereafter." George then released his friend and rubbed the thatch on his head.

John said nothing but embraced Ingram and then turned away. As Ingram settled himself on the wagon, he brushed across his good eye with the sleeve to his gown.

"Right then, we're off." Brother Martin shook the reins and the wagon lurched away.

Once more, Ingram appeared to be the plaything of fate. No sooner had he set foot on French soil than he learned that the great master had since gone to perform music in the very presence of his Maker. A letter to that effect had passed him on the waters. Brother Martin, who unsealed it, delivered the news to Robert. Hurried arrangements were made so that Ingram could return to Edinburgh to study with William Roger, the royal musician. Abbot Henry agreed to support the boy's study under the original terms.

From the brief and infrequent letters he sent back to his masters, Ingram seemed content enough. In writing of his young pupils, he marveled at Brother Martin's infinite well of patience. He boasted of Master Roger's unrelenting demands for perfections and hinted at relations with Master Thomas Cochrane, a powerful man at court, who had the royal ear and who could bend other men's fortunes to his will. These allayed Robert and Martin's fears that the world outside Dunfermline would swallow the boy whole.

The designated three years passed, then four. It became apparent that Ingram's absence was to be extended indefinitely by the good pleasure of the king. To mollify Abbot Crichton for the abbey's lost revenues, James wrote:

> We are certain that you, our dear brother in Christ, will under-stand our great affection for Ingram Bannatyne, our loyal servant, and of our urgent need and sincerest desire that he assist our chief musician, William Roger, in our residence at Holyrood. We there-fore ask that you pardon his absence and release him from the bond into which he entered prior to undertaking his studies with Master William.

James made certain of the abbot's understanding, pardon, and release by deeding to the abbey certain lands in Fife.

After a six-year absence, Ingram returned to Dunfermline. The trans-formation could not have been greater. He had grown nearly an inch for every year he had been away, and the boyish weight had either disap-peared or been stretched with his height. Nothing could diminish the size of his ears, but a bonnet softened the exaggeration and covered, if not tamed, the unruly hair. A silk eyepatch, along with the bonnet, lent him a gallant, almost roguish air. "Handsome" was a word that was never going to describe him, but he had learned to work with what he had and he now carried himself with dignity. As he walked the corridor to the *camera musicum*, the young choristers nodded in respect to his fur-trimmed gown.

"Here, let us look at you." Brother Martin held him at arm's length after first embracing him. "Court wine and court food have agreed with him, wouldn't you say?" Martin turned to Robert, who was waiting his turn to greet his former pupil.

"Aye." Ingram smiled. "And a French damsel."

When Martin stiffened, Ingram winked to Robert. "I'm to be married, Brother Martin. To Agnes Beauchamp, one of the Queen's maids-in-wait-ing. It was Master Robert's French that won her heart."

Brother Martin pulled him close. "I suppose you are old enough to know your own mind." There were tears in the old man's eyes. "I had ever thought you would be minstrel to Mother Church."

"And so I shall." Ingram sought to re-assure his former master. "There are places enough to sing her praise at the court of King Jamie."

Robert was silent throughout, studying Ingram and Brother Martin all the while. Six years had worked nearly as great a transformation in the older man. Nearly seventy now, he had grown feebler. Still, he refused the abbot's yearly offer of an assistant. Robert now knew why. Martin cherished the notion that his star pupil might return as his assistant and eventually the choirmaster. Into no other hands would he entrust the future of the abbey's music. Ingram could not be blamed for falsely encouraging the old man. He had given no indication whatsoever that he would ever return. It was just that now, with this announcement of his impending marriage, Brother Martin understood the fixity of Ingram's plans.

"Are you all right, Brother Martin?"

"Aye, lad. Pay no mind to the foolish tears of an old man. I could hardly to be more proud. It's King James I'm envying." Martin dabbed at his eyes. "Will you not treat us to your music this evening?"

Ingram nodded. Both Martin and Robert made to leave. Ingram reached for Robert's arm. "Might I speak with you, Master Robert?"

"I'll see you both in the refectory presently." Martin seemed glad for an excuse to carry his emotion away from so public a view.

"It's good to see you again," Robert said when he and Ingram were alone.

"You're not angry with me for not writing more often?"

Robert brushed away the suggestion. "As long as you were well." He added, "You were well?"

"Not at first, as you must have imagined, tossed between Scotland and France and back again. Then to learn how much of my misery I brought upon myself." Ingram smiled at Robert's silent assent.

Robert smiled in return. "What made you stay?"

"I could not leave. Perhaps it was the gift you spoke of, demanding that I see it through. I would have always regretted my leaving."

"And Roger?"

"Arrogant beyond words. He quickly gave me to learn that I could never inflict as much misery on myself as he could, so I should cease trying. But his music—" Ingram truly did lose his words at that moment, but his wonder was tinged with sadness.

Robert sensed that Ingram wished to say more, but the moment must have passed. Like his former choirmaster, Ingram was overcome by an emotion of his own. Robert released him from his embarrassment. "Come,

50

let us dine."

Ingram did sing for the brothers after vespers that evening. Master Roger had found in that ethereal contratenor a rich soil in which a garden of delicately varied sounds might bloom. Hints of pain and sorrow still lingered there. In what life would they not ever do so? But the world for Ingram also looked brighter.

Play he did as well, the gittern, as in former days. It was one of his own purchasing, lavishly carved with scrollwork like that in a lady's breviary. Robert glanced over at Martin and saw that the old man had closed his eyes. He was smiling.

"What was it you heard, then?" Robert asked, as he and Martin made their way afterwards to their cells.

"It was as fine a piece of singing as any I've ever heard—or am like to hear, either. He's a bit too enamored of the Englishman's effects."

Robert had feared that Ingram might be dazzled, if not completely blinded, by the spangles of courtly finery and the elegance of courtly manners and the clever embellishments of courtly music. Martin had no such fears. "It is his youth. There's time enough for him to find his own voice, and age will season him. As it is, I could not have brought him to this point, never in a lifetime."

Ingram returned to court. He continued to enjoy the favor of Roger and Cochrane and the king himself. His marriage to Agnes bore fruit almost immediately, giving the lie to his fellows' comments about his cullions. Within a year he was a father and just months later, when Robert saw him that evening in late 1481, another was on the way.

"Court life agrees ever more greatly." Robert smiled when Ingram came to greet him at his table.

Ingram patted a bloated stomach. "My dame Agnes' cook. Come, lass, be known to my old teacher and the guest of honor tonight: Master Robert of Dunfermline." He pulled to his side a small creature, barely five feet tall, whose stomach swelled ever so slightly. She was not a third of Ingram's size, or so it seemed. In her curtsey and finery, Robert could read the signs of one bred as the daughter of a wealthy French burgess. It was clear that Ingram adored her.

"Not like John over there. He's gained never an ounce of flesh in all this time." Ingram pointed toward his old schoolmate. Robert followed the direction of Ingram's stubby fingers to a corner of the hall where a slight, bent figure was speaking earnestly to a man elegantly clad and wearing an impressive chain of office. The latter seemed to be brushing aside either the counsel or the presence of the former, or both.

"He speaks with Thomas Cochrane, the chancellor. No doubt John makes some petition on behalf of the Earl of Angus, his master."

Robert studied the two men. Cochrane, a former stonemason, was tall, well over six feet, and massive, like the Great Hall whose construction he supervised and in which they now ate. Next to him, John seemed frail and inconsequential. Robert's limited and primarily literary exposure to life at court had suggested that a man in Cochrane's position would be a fawning character: officious, eager to do the king's bidding, swift to detect the slightest change in the winds of court favor. But Cochrane's face and demeanor told a far different story. The face was not haughty, stern, or even cold, but politely impassive. He carried himself with grace and obviously felt at ease in these surroundings, having long been accustomed to giving orders and shaping the tastes of nobility and royalty as well as stone. Here was no toady, but a man capable of exerting a profound influence, either for good or bad. With his blessing, a seed of promise might be nurtured to flowering. His enmity, however, might grind that same seed to meal. Robert determined that men far nobler in birth might make or break themselves on Lord Chancellor Cochrane.

Robert turned back to Ingram. "So you and John have remained friends?"

Ingram gently patted Agnes off to her place at board. "Aye. For years we seldom saw one another, what with his being at university. But when he returned from Glasgow to the employ of the Earl of Angus, we crossed paths at court. He's godfather to our young Rebecca." Ingram cast an affectionate look in John's direction. John happened to straighten up at the moment. Frustration and annoyance clouded his face. The frown lightened when he saw Ingram; and when he recognized the one to whom Ingram was speaking, he even allowed himself to smile.

Ingram settled himself on a nearby bench. With the ease of one who had found his place in the world, he pointed out the persons of note in the room, sometimes adding a bit of comfortable gossip.

"That will be Archibald, the Sixth Earl of Angus, at that table there. John landed on cat's feet when he obtained that appointment. The Angus is the greatest magnate in the realm. At the next table are the Lords Crichton and Gray; and over there are Sir John Douglas, and Alexander Home. Bishop Laing of Glasgow perhaps you'll have already seen. And of course Archbishop Scheves, who preached at this evening's service. Even now, some eight years since, the other churchmen chafe under the pope's decision to make St. Andrews an archbishopric, and Scheves has done little to salve the irritation."

Robert nodded. This decision, no doubt with a great deal of politicking by Scheves, was often food for conversation at the abbey. As abbot, Henry Crichton owed ecclesiastical allegiance to no one, bishop or archbishop, only to to the pope. But as a member of the powerful Crichton family, he had definite opinions about Scheves' accumulation of power.

"And next to the archbishop?" Robert asked. A lean figure, clothed in a dark gown trimmed in gray rabbit's fur, was making a studied effort to talk to everyone but Scheves.

"A great doctor of the Church and a son of Scotland," Ingram replied. "John of Ireland, now in service to the French king, Louis XI. Dr. John and the good archbishop can barely hide their contempt for one another. They were at St. Andrews together—" Ingram lowered his voice and laid his finger next to his nose— "and there are stories...." Ingram took a tankard from a passing tray. "Tell me, what did you think of the Mass?"

"Archbishop Scheves' sermon gave much to ponder." Robert knew what Ingram angled for, but the teacher was too old a fish to be quickly caught.

Ingram could not hide his disappointment. "And the music? What did you think of the music?"

"Master Roger's work, I take it? A bit too English for my taste, but he's quite talented. I'll begrudge him that praise." When Ingram's face fell, Robert released him from his torment. "I knew your handiwork immediately. I've never before heard the like. My heart overflowed with joy and, I confess, with pride."

"Did you indeed find it too English?"

"Not a bit."

Ingram sighed in relief.

Robert added, "I was merely scourging your pride."

"I did not want to disappoint you."

"It's not a matter of disappointing. You've so far passed our expectations, every new piece simply adds to our wonder. But here now, tell me about the piece."

Ingram launched into a detailed explanation of his Mass. "I developed it upon 'L'homme armé.' It's a popular tune."

"I know. Father Ninian, my old priest in Edinburgh, who fought alongside James II, used to hum it."

"You'll remember the Mass that Jacques de l'Isle conducted before Abbot Henry and the French ambassador—the one by Guillaume Dufay?"

"Aye."

"I modeled mine after his."

"And Master Roger did not mind?"

Ingram looked confused.

"That yours was so French?"

Ingram laughed. "Music knows no kingdoms for him, English, Scots, even French. Besides, it is for Mother Church, not some earthly master, I sing."

Robert studied the face of his pupil closely. He saw there no trace of mockery or arrogance. "Aye," he replied, "I believe you do."

Ingram's attentions were drawn past Robert. "Ah, the Master of Royal Entertainments, our George, has given me the signal to sing. Pardon me for leaving you." He rose and bowed. Robert nodded and patted his arm.

After ascending the performers' dais, Ingram looked in the direction of Robert and smiled. He then began to sing. The words Robert knew intimately. They were his own "Bloody Shirt" now set to music.

> This year just past I heard it told
> There was a worthy king:
> Dukes and earls and barons bold
> He had at his bidding.
> The lord was ancient and old
> And sixty years had reigned.
> He had a daughter fair in fold,
> A lusty lady young.
>
> Of womanhood she bore the flower
> And was her father's heir;
> Of graces true and high honor,
> Both meek and debonair.
> She lived within a handsome bower
> On earth was none so fair.
> Princes loved her, paramour,
> In countries everywhere.

Robert felt a hand on his shoulder. John had threaded his way through the ever-shifting mass of servants trying to satisfy the voracious demands of the diners. "He wrote it especially for this occasion," John whispered. "In your honor."

VII

The Trial of the Fox

"Robert." Charles was bending over the sleeping figure, lightly shaking his shoulder. "Robert. Abbot George and the notary are here, as you requested. You wanted to make out your testament?"

"Uhm." Robert stirred. He had tossed fitfully through the night and had only a short time before drifted off into a sound sleep. The pain in his stomach had become more severe. After having prayed for a stay of execution until his fables were finished, he now wished for death to come quickly. He opened one eye to see the familiar grin.

"I'm sorry to disturb your slumber, but some of us have work to do."

Robert mustered enough strength to grumble. "O, aye. Come to find your own name among the beneficiaries."

"You're feeling better, I see, Master Robert." Robert looked beyond Charles to see Abbot George smiling. "Father Charles has that effect on many of the infirm brothers. They get better when he approaches just to avoid his 'ministrations.' Still, just to be on the safe side, perhaps it were better that we do make out your testament. For my own part, I'd be loath to let slip your books from our grasp here at the abbey."

Robert grunted. "Vultures, the lot of you. Circling even before my body ceases to twitch." He sat up slowly, and Charles helped him to arrange his pillows. Robert finally noticed the younger man in the room. "Do I know you?" he asked.

"John Asloan, Master Robert. I was one of your students nearly ten years since."

"Like yourself, Master Robert, a licentiate in civil and canon law from Glasgow." George broke in. "He's a notary and scribe here in the burgh. A fine hand he has."

Robert squinted at the young man. "Ah yes. I recognize you now. John, or rather Master John. I'm sorry; my eyes are not what they used to be, especially at any distance."

"Too many late nights reading by dim candlelight," Charles scolded, "or scratching out your verse."

The notary had settled himself at Robert's writing desk, and George coughed lightly. "Whenever you are ready, Master Robert."

With the ease that comes from years of familiarity, Robert began to speak the words he had recorded for so many others who found themselves in his condition:

> *In nomine Patri, Filii, et Spiritu Sancti, Amen.* The thirteenth day of August in the sixteenth year of the reign of our most gracious Sovereign King James, fourth by that name, by the grace of God of Scotland. And in the year of our Lord God one thousand five hundred and four.

> I, Robert Henryson, schoolmaster of Dunfermline, being of whole mind and in good and perfect remembrance, praise be unto Almighty God, make and ordain this, my present testament containing herein my last will in manner and form following.

Robert could hear the scratching of John's quill. He began to list his few moveables. If his testament were to read aright, he would little care what happened to most of his books, which he once counted his treasures. Only the thought of parting with his Troilus book, the gift of Alexander Inglis, his one-time employer, gave him the slightest twinge of grief. No, it was other things he would bequeathe—had already bequeathed—that he would set down, less as a testament than as a hope and a wish that his life had not been in vain. His own poetry, the lives of his students. By these his life would be measured, and he feared the measurement would be uneven.

But one does not list the essence of poems or the memory of lives as objects in a will.

Item. Boethius' *De musica* to my godson, Robert, second child of Ingram Bannatyne. Though he sings just as badly as you, Charles.

"You'll not be wanting me to add that phrase, I trust," John said.

"Nay." Robert smiled. Robert Bannatyne, who had been born after his father's death, had inherited nothing of Ingram's angelic voice nor, for that matter, his looks. Instead, he had his mother's administrative gifts and her taste for the exquisite. He had thus landed himself a choice position as steward of the Bothwell family, which had taken over the forfeited estates of Lord Crichton. Robert was overseeing the refurbishing of the entire castle. He would treasure the *De musica*. It would appeal to his sense of order in the universe.

Item. To Abbot George Crichton, Cicero's *De officiis*, much annotated.

George little needed Cicero to guide him in his duties. He had long ago committed much of the Roman's teaching to memory and practice. No, this gift was a testimony to Robert's affection for the man. George bowed his head in gratitude.

Item. To my dearest friend and brother in Christ, Father Charles Braidwod, I bequeathe my Troilus book, that as one who never succumbed to Fortune's blandishments, he might be trustee over the story of those who did.

Charles took his hand.

As Robert listed his meager possessions, his mind could hear a boy's voice—the voice of another John—reading another list, almost as meager.

Item. Twelve wooden slates.
Item. Fifteen charcoals, the which to write upon the slates.
Item. One inkwell for the master.
Item. Three goose quills for the master.

The boy stopped reading. He was tall, slight, angular—even bony—

and, with an intensity that was almost palpable. Abbot Henry had sent him with the inventory to the classroom, where Robert was preparing for the upcoming term.

"That is the complete list?" Robert asked.

"Aye."

"And the books? Are there no books?"

"None that I find here. This is all Abbot Henry gave me." He handed over the parchment from which he read. Robert eyed it carefully.

"Why not?"

"They did not, it seems, belong to the school, but to Master Cuthbert's brother, a merchant in York—"

Robert muttered something under his breath about treasures in a dung-heap.

"My father's a merchant, sir."

"O aye?"

"Aye."

It was all Robert could do to contain his irritation at the shabby condition of the school. Brother Cuthbert was an ancient fixture about the place when Abbot Henry had arrived. Knowing that it was simply a matter of a few years, if not months, before age took the old schoolmaster off, Henry had chosen to bide his time. Providence was kind. Within two years of Henry's promotion, the old schoolmaster was dead.

But Cuthbert was not the senile old man he appeared to be in his later years. Throughout his long career, he had drawn upon the devotion and the wealth of his younger brother, the York merchant, to endow the school with books and parchment. It was, of course, expected that when Cuthbert died, this small, but select library would revert to the monastery. Cuthbert, however, was a long-time friend of Alexander Thomson, Henry's rival for the abbacy. In protest against Henry's appointment, Cuthbert persuaded his merchant brother to take back into his own possession all the books and supplies he had lavishly bestowed on the school throughout all those years. The brother had obliged and donated them to an English foundation. Robert could appreciate Cuthbert's anger and frustration, but to cause the boys to suffer? To appreciate the decision was one thing; pardoning was quite another.

He shook off his distraction. None of this was the boy's fault. "Then tell me about your father. And your mother, too."

"He's a vintner, sir. Father Charles purchases much of the abbey's stock of wines from him."

"Richard de Leith. Father Charles has told me of your father. And of you."

In one of their early conversations, Charles had spoken of Richard's wealth and shrewd ways. "He's an honest man, but hard, and always calculating how much even a farthing will buy him. John is much more agreeable. Cuthbert praised him as perhaps the brightest boy he had ever taught. But," he had added, "the father has great aspirations for his son. I fear the pressure on the boy is very great." Charles tapped his forefinger on his temple. "Richard knows why Henry was appointed abbot and is eager that John establish connections with the Crichton family. That's why the boy did not go home for the summer recess. Richard would use him to gain valuable influence."

The boy continued. "It occurs to me that my father could make a gift of books—to replace the ones that Master Cuthbert's brother took away."

Robert could have bitten his tongue about the treasure-in-a-dungheap remark.

"Does your father like books?"

"He likes to possess books. And he likes what they can do for me."

"And that is?"

"My father wishes me to make a name for myself."

"As a merchant?"

"Aye."

"You need no great schooling to be a merchant, even a distinguished one."

"He knows that, sir. It's a matter of pride with him." The boy seemed hesitant.

"And you? Do you wish to make a name for yourself as a merchant?"

"Begging your pardon, sir. Might we speak frankly?"

"Aye. Tell me your mind."

"I wish to go into the law."

Robert hesitated before he spoke next. "A father's blessing is not to be taken lightly." He was thinking of his own father and wondered if the dead plowman would have blessed his son's choices.

"No sir."

"You would risk displeasing him?"

John evaded the question. "You were a procurator, were you not?"

"Aye."

"And are you not also a notary?"

"That also."

As John expelled a deep sigh, he hunched his narrow shoulders Indeed, he seemed almost to shrivel. It took him a moment to gather the strength to continue. "In his eagerness for me to learn the ways of the trade, Father took me to sessions of the burgh court, where his cases were heard and his contracts made. He has a name among the other burgesses in Leith for his ability—and eagerness—to squeeze a merk from a shilling and a pound from a merk." Here, he paused, as if judging how much he should tell this man whom he hardly knew.

"And some poor souls have been squeezed likewise, is that it?"

"O, not by outright deceit or by the breaking of the law." By the speed with which John replied, he obviously feared that he might bring a curse upon this man he certainly loved but could not bring himself to admire.

"But?"

John hung his head. "But by pressing every claim and snapping up every sasine born of someone else's distress." John raised his head and looked Robert directly in the eye. "I would not live like that."

"Nor need you, were you to become a merchant."

"I do not wish to leave in need those whom my father made more desperate."

The words sounded only too familiar. Robert, whose own early aspirations were shaped by similar ideals, warned him of what lay ahead. "The law is a treacherous country. Its forests are dense and the clearest paths often lead to deadly marshes."

"I would learn. I would have you teach me."

It was Robert's turn to sigh. "You have much to do before you even reach that country. I can help you chart your course. But have you the will to follow it?"

The boy straightened his shoulders and through the effort they and seemed to broaden. "Aye," he said simply. Because of that one word, Robert decided to gamble the precious moments that teaching John would entail.

"We shall begin tomorrow."

"Thank you, sir." John spoke the words as if entering into a contract. He knew the labor Robert had just promised to incur and meant to satisfy, nay, exceed, his terms of the bargain.

Just as John was about to excuse himself, Robert said, "Perhaps we can talk to your father about some books?"

John grinned. "Aye."

When alone again, Robert surveyed one more time the desolate schoolroom, then set himself to more profitable thoughts. If it were the law John would learn, it was the law Robert would teach him in ways that were fitting for a lad of fourteen. He padded back to the oratory of his cell, where as yet his books lay in stacks until Walter, a lay brother and the abbey's carpenter, could make him some shelves.

He took out his old protocol books and mentally noted those entries that he would later copy to demonstrate to John the range of his activities as a notary. As he did so he was struck with an idea. He remembered entertaining the Inglis children to some of his versions of Aesop's fables. Such fables, depicting as they often did the conflicting interests between animals, lent themselves well to embellishment with legal terminology and procedure. He had but to set them within a Scottish landscape.

A month or so remained before the other boys arrived, so in the evenings, after days of haggling with Abbot Henry about funds for the school, of negotiating with Richard de Leith for a donation of books, and the occasional drink with Father Charles, Robert began to work on the fable he had selected to begin John's instruction. Some two weeks later, when John appeared in the schoolroom, Robert handed him a fair copy of the finished work.

"Read it," Robert commanded, "aloud."

John read of a royal summons issued by a unicorn: "With horn in hand, a box on breast he bore; A pursuivant seemly, I you assure."

"The pursuivant is?" Robert interrupted.

"A junior member in the court of the Lord Lyon King-of-Arms. One of which," John added, "is the Unicorn Pursuivant."

Robert nodded his approval.

"Oyas! Oyas!"

"With fervor!" Robert shouted. "No one is going to answer the summons of a herald who speaks in such a tender voice. Again."

"Oyas! Oyas!"

"Louder."

"Oyas! Oyas!"

"Much better. Read on."

John smiled and continued.

> "We, noble Lyon, of all beasts the king,
> Greeting in God, eterne, without ending,
> To all brute beasts and irrational
> I send, as to my subjectis great and small."

"All legal documents have preambles such as this." Robert interrupted again. "Notaries and clerks have formularies with examples to draw upon."

> "My celsitude and high magnificence
> Lets you to know that even incontinent
> We think this morn, with royal diligence,
> Upon this hill to hold a parliament.
> Straightly, therefore, I give commandment
> That all compear before my tribunal,
> Under all pain and peril that may fall."

Another interruption. "This is a judicial parliament, one called to try notorious malefactors." Robert, it seemed, was going to comment on nearly every stanza.

John plodded ahead, naming the beasts who assembled. There were, of course, the common animals one might expect: dogs, birds, horses deer, goats, sheep, swine, rats, mice, asses, mules, beavers, hedgehogs, hares, otters, porcupines, bears, and bulls. Joining their ranks, however, were more exotic creatures: a lynx, a tiger, an elephant, a camel, an antelope, a reindeer, and an ape. Even some fabulous beasts—Pegasus, the flying horse, a minotaur, and a werewolf—were thrown in for good measure.

Lyon opened the court by bidding his subjects not to be afraid but to stand on their feet:

> "I let you know, my might is merciful
> And stirs gainst none that are to me prostrate;
> But angry, stern, austere, unamiable
> To those who bow no knees to mine estate."

The king's justiciar then "fenced" the courts, calling forth suits, and forfeiting all those who were absent. A fox lurking nearby realized at once that the court had been called to "attach" such as he with past crimes of theft or even treason. Yet, to the surprise of everyone, the King appointed him an officer of the court, charged with summoning an absent mare for "contumacy." The wolf—one "cunning in clergy," with "great practice of the chancery"—was to accompany him.

To summon the mare was one thing. To bring her back to court was another. She argued that she had, imprinted on her hoof, a "respite" exempting her from attending the parliament. The fox pleaded illiteracy and deferred to the wolf, who received a bloody crown for his efforts.

John laughed out loud.

"Go on," Robert urged.

Success in tempting fate once lured the fox to commit a bolder crime, killing a lamb. The mother of the dead lamb appeared and accused the fox of murder, pointing to the evidence: "Thy gory gums and thy bloody snout—The wool, the flesh, yet sticks upon thy teeth."

The King's justiciar called a new assize, which, as might be expected, convicted the fox of murder and theft. But to these charges was added treason, since he had killed the lamb within a mile of the King's person. After doom was pronounced, the fox was led to the gallows, where the ape carried out the execution.

After John finished reading, Robert informed him that a *moralitas*, or lesson, would follow at some point. "But you get some sense now of how the king's court in parliament and justice ayres proceed."

"Will you write some more fables?"

"For now, we will examine real documents."

More pressing matters intervened, and the requested fables never found their way to paper. But each week, John appeared at Robert's cell and, after a time, became something of an unofficial secretary, helping to arrange for binding parchments that still lay piled in corners months after Walter had built the shelves.

One morning, as John was sorting through the chaos, he came across a legal instrument that made him pause. "Master Robert?"

"What is it?" Robert was collating another stack.

"I recognized a name here."

"Aye?"

"George Kincaid."

"Here, let me see." Robert read over the document.

> *In Dei nomine,* Amen.
>
> I, George Kincaid, bailie of the barony of Brouchton, within the sheriffdom of Edinburgh, to John Galbraith, sergeant of the said barony, Greeting.
>
> I charge and I command thee that these my letters by thee seen, thou pass without delay to the tolbooth lying within my said barony, and there thou summon lawfully before sufficient witnesses Alice Napier, spouse of the deceased Allen Douglas, that

calls herself tenant of the acre of land in St. Leonard's Gate, between the half acre of John Creniston on the south and the half acre of Adam Gray on the north, lying within the said barony. To compear at the tolbooth within the said barony, before me, the baron-baillie of the said tenantry in my court there to be held in the tolbooth the tenth day of the month of May, the year of God one thousand four hundred and threescore years and eight, for to show to me her holding, her charter, and evidences, if she any has, how and by what title of right and for what service she claims to hold the tenantry of the said acre of Sir Roger Logan, laird of the said barony.

And be thou there the said day and place with this precept, thy summons, and witnesses, and this on nowise thou leave undone under all charge that thou may incur a loss concerning me in that part.

Written under my signet, at Brouchton, the first day of the month of April, the year of God 1468.

"I vaguely remember the matter. How would you know anything about George Kincaid? You would not have been more than seven or eight."

Instead of answering, John asked to see Robert's protocol book from the period, a record of all the transactions that Robert had witnessed and certified. He came across the corresponding entry.

Instrument narrating that Andrew Ross, as prolocutor for Richard de Leith and Janet Menzies, his spouse, compeared before George Kincaid, bailie of the barony of Brouchton, and declared that Alice Napier, spouse of the deceased Allen Douglas, had resigned in the hands of William, the deceased abbot of Holyrood, an acre of land in St. Leonard's Gate, between the half acre of John Creniston on the south and the half acre of Adam Gray on the north, and that the said Richard de Leith and his spouse were in possession of the said acre through resignation by the said William, abbot of Holyrood, in whose favor the said Alice had resigned the said acre; notwithstanding that the said Alice, appearing in her own person, swore that she had, in presence of Archibald of Holyroodhouse, revoked her said resignation. Done in the tolbooth of Brouchton, 10 May 1468.

Witnesses:

George Kincaid, bailie of the barony of Brouchton

John Galbraith, sergeant of the said barony

Alexander Preston, John Home, and Adam Wedderburn, burgesses of the said barony

Deans James Forman and John Wright, canons of the said monastery

"Is this Richard your father, then?"

"Aye. Can you tell me what happened?"

Robert thought for a time, trying to recollect the details of the case and the circumstances of his involvement. At the time, he was still acting as William Cunningham's assistant procurator, besides serving as notary in some of the Border communities around Peebles, including Brouchton. It was in the latter capacity that he had acted in the case of Alice Napier. He had learned then how vulnerable the law was to abuse, especially in a baron's court, where one such as George Kincaid, acting with the full consent of his superior, Sir Roger Logan, had nearly unrestrained power.

"Alice Napier could not have been much beyond thirty. She came to the tollbooth, a wee creature, but with a strapping son, some twelve years old, and a bairn hardly weaned in arms. She seemed so frail in the midst of those imposing men, who had done everything to make themselves more imposing."

"So you took her case?"

"Having notarized the proceedings against her, I could not but fail to see the sorry plight she was in."

"What put her in that condition?"

"Allen Douglas—"

"The husband?"

"Aye. He had agreed to render feu service in lieu of rent, but died suddenly, before he could carry the service out. With the rent in arrears, Kincaid saw this as a chance to cause the land to revert to his lairdship and thus increase the rents. Alice, who held the property in liferent, appealed to the abbot of Holyrood for assistance. She temporarily resigned the acre to Abbot William in exchange for the rent, with the understanding that her son would work for the abbey to repay the debt."

"And did he?"

"He never got the opportunity. Abbot William died and his successor, the Abbot Archibald, claimed to know nothing of the arrangement."

"But was nothing written?"

"Nay. The poor woman was ignorant of the law. Besides, she believed she could trust Mother Church. She appeared before Abbot Archibald's assistant to revoke the resignation. It was duly recorded, but the debt still remained. Shortly thereafter, the abbey resigned to property to Richard de Leith and Janet Menzies. I little suspected that they were your parents."

"My father was often doing business with the abbey. He was the chief importer of their wines and knew Abbot Archibald for a long time prior to his appointment."

"No doubt there was ample consideration all around. The burgh court found in favor of your father."

"What happened to the family?"

"My Master Cunningham settled them in Peebles out of his own funds. The son was apprenticed to a fletcher."

"There's a great need of arrows, what with all the fighting in the Borders. By now it's certain he's left his mark in many an English carcass."

Robert smiled sadly, thinking to himself of his own childhood, "and a Scottish reiver or two, no doubt." Out loud he said, "They lived for a time on Alice's mending and sewing, but not so well off as they would have been." Even with Cunningham's aid, the inexperienced Robert had been routed by the legal forces arrayed against him. Partly to relieve Alice from the burdens she then faced and partly to relieve his own shame, he had anonymously sent the family a portion of his income until Alice remarried some two years after.

"So you never met my father?" John asked.

"Nay. Neither of the principals—your father or Sir Roger—had any direct hand in the matter. Nor the abbot of Holyrood, for that matter, until some time later." Robert paused, then added. "He broke no law, your father."

"Small comfort to those like Alice Napier," John answered.

This was true, Robert agreed. Snapping up forfeited or resigned parcels of land was common practice. A person of means need never know the circumstances of such reversions—that was the work of his procurator or factor. The law could perfume the most grasping of hands. Even a moment's pause and the owner of such a hand would have to realize that the property he plucked was the fruit of someone else's misery and grief. These were busy times, however, and allowed for few such reflections.

There were expenses to be paid, profits to be made.

"There ought to be laws in such cases." John set his jaw.

"Perhaps. But remember your Cicero."

"Aye," John replied, "'*summum ius summa iniuria*.'" This was one of the first maxims from the Roman orator's *De officiis* that Robert instilled in his pupil. "More law, more injustice."

"And more lawyers." Robert winked. He then grew serious. "The law is of no force unless this"—he pointed to John's heart—"is joined to this." He laid his hand on the boy's head as if in benediction. John shuddered. "Unless the heart guide the head to reflect, this"—here he poked John's thin belly—"will govern all. The head will simply devise more reasons and more intricate means to enlarge the stomach's domain." Robert pinched at John's waist. There was little enough to catch hold of. "Your heart has been doing its proper work. No one can accuse your stomach of greed." He tousled John's head. "Back to work. Here, at least, in my wee cell, you can bring some order to the world."

A year later, John left for the University of Glasgow with every intention of following Robert's path. Indeed, he so distinguished himself in his legal studies that when he graduated as a licentiate, the chancellor of the university invited him to join the law faculty. But his efforts had also brought him to the attention of another chancellor, the Chancellor of Scotland, Robert Laing, Bishop of Glasgow.

John sent the following letter to his schoolmaster.

> You will perhaps have forgotten our conversation about my father and poor Alice Napier. It has, however, stalked my memory these six years. Bishop Laing has procured for me a position as keeper of the signet and personal secretary to Archibald Douglas, the Earl of Angus.
>
> I greatly desire your blessing on this appointment. His lordship, as you well know, is one of the principle men in the realm, capable of doing much good and much mischief in the lives of the Napiers of this kingdom. My sincerest prayer is that I might keep his conscience as well as his signet.
>
> Yours, ever humbly and gratefully,
> John de Leith, Lic. juris canonici & civili

Robert was eager to grant his blessing, but also wished to lay out for

John the dangers of the course he was taking. His opportunity came in early 1481 when John made a detour to Dunfermline on his journey from Glasgow to Tantallon Castle near North Berwick, the home of the Earl of Angus.

"Come in, come in," Robert welcomed his former student. "Here, let me look at you."

John spun around to display his gown to its full effect. He came to a stop facing his master and posed with his fists on his hips. Robert clapped at the mock bravado. "A drink to celebrate your good fortune, perhaps?"

The two men walked together from the abbey to the Lion and Mouse, a tavern in the center of the burgh. As they passed through the high street, merchants and tradesmen doffed their hats and their good wives curtsied. A number of the younger women, Robert noticed, went out of their way to show courtesy to the striking young man at his side.

Inside the tavern, Robert raised a toast. "To the newly minted master."

John smiled and clapped Robert's tankard with his own. "*Magistro magistorum*. To the master of masters."

"No one could be prouder of your achievements and your appointment than I." Robert took a drink. "Unless it be your father."

"Aye, he's proud enough."

"And he's not upset that you will not be taking over the family business?"

"How can he be? He stands to gain new custom from the Angus estates. The Earl is fond of his claret. Father Charles would be hard pressed to match him, glass for glass."

"I would have invited Father Charles to join us, but my purse is not sufficiently ample." Robert smiled. He then changed the subject to something that had been on his mind since he had received John's letter. "When last you wrote, you requested my blessing about your new position."

"Aye. And I was serious."

"Serious or not, you received my blessing when first I heard your news; and I have assailed the Kingdom of Heaven with my prayers that the Holy Spirit grant you wisdom, courage, and tact. I would not put this in writing, but the affairs of state are like mighty waves, and such men as the Earl of Angus treacherous rocks whose greatest dangers lurk hidden from view. A man might be swimming along well away from the harm he sees only to be crushed against what lies beneath. The earl is not over fond of the king."

"And has little reason, given that the king revoked lands and titles previously awarded to the Angus and conferred them upon those less worthy."

John's voice had an edge to it.

"You've become a partisan of the Angus already?"

John relaxed. "I'm sorry, Master Robert."

Robert patted his arm. "Hence my prayers. Come. You've paid your respects to Abbot Henry?"

"Aye."

"Then we'll see Father Charles."

So it was that, less than a year later, Robert found himself sitting next to John at the royal banquet in Stirling, applauding Ingram's music with the enthusiastic court. "He is in his element here," John said, when the clapping subsided. "You'll remember how few friends he had at the abbey school."

"None that I know, besides you and George."

"Here he's adored. The ladies make a great to-do about him and laugh when Dame Agnes scolds him for paying too much attention. I suspect he—and Agnes—know that he's no threat to maidenhead."

"And you? No damoiselle has caught your heart?"

John blushed. "My eye, now and then, but not my heart."

Robert reached out and fingered the great chain that hung from John's neck and inspected the heraldic device on the signet. "A fess chequy surmounted by a bend charged with three buckles. Has this caught your heart, instead, or your soul?"

"Nay, it'll not be so strong a chain as all that, though heavy enough."

"Have my prayers been answered then?"

John bent over and whispered. "His lordship is a willful man, and the claret does little but fuel his choler. He nurses wrongs—real or imagined— as if they were his children. Would the king not flaunt so boldly his favors to his low-born attendants."

"Like Ingram? Or even George?"

"Please don't misconstrue my meaning. The gifts to Cochrane and some of the others are out of all proportion to their talents. Besides, the king seems to delight in provoking my master."

"Hence, your frown a moment ago."

John sighed. "Aye. The earl sent me to request an audience with the king tomorrow. Chancellor Cochrane intercepted me and informed me that his highness will be hunting with some of his other guests the whole day. I've discovered that my master himself is not above provoking. He'll ask of the king unreasonable favors or inconvenient meetings."

"You've not told the earl of the chancellor's reply."

"Nay, I came to see you first. His lordship knew the king's answer, even before I asked. He'll not press me until the morrow."

"What will you tell him?"

"I'll do my best to ease his anger."

John looked up and at that moment, Robert felt a hand on his shoulder. George spoke. "Please forgive my interruption, but the queen requests that Master Robert read now."

John rose. "Pray for me, Master Robert."

"Fervently," Robert replied. "I often do."

They shook hands, and John walked stiffly to the table where the Earl of Angus was holding his own small court and regaling his guests with some story or other. Robert observed him glance ever so slightly and ever so briefly in John's direction as if to read his secretary's mood. He seemed to be satisfied with what he found there and turned back to his companions. He had not quit speaking all the while. In the time it took to follow George to the small stage, Robert did offer a brief prayer, two, to be precise. One of petition, as John had requested. The other of thanksgiving, that Providence had placed one such as John close to the ear of Angus.

VIII

The Lion and the Mouse

Item. I give to the Hospital of St. Luke the Physician in Stirling ten merks.

Item. I give to the Abbey of Christ Church and the Holy Trinity, Dunfermline, the residue of my earthly possessions.

Finally, I commend my soul unto Almighty God, my maker, to the Lord Jesu Christ, my Redeemer, and to the Blessed Virgin Mary. And my body to be buried in the Abbey Churchyard of Dunfermline or else where it shall please God.

Robert finished dictating the will and John, the notary, brought the document over to the bedside. As he did so, Robert removed the signet ring from his finger. When John daubed hot wax at the bottom of the will, Robert impressed the ring into the wax.

"This seems straightforward enough." Abbot George assumed a terse official manner as a defense against his emotion. "We will let you rest, now, Master Robert." He, Charles, and John slipped out.

Robert must have slept a long time, because he awoke to the sound of boys shouting outside. The angle of the sun through the oratory window told him it was the late afternoon.

"Must get up. Order my affairs." Robert rose, steadied himself, and slowly made his way to his desk. "Not much more now." He began to sort through leaves of manuscript that lay scattered throughout the room. Charles had found only a part of his work on the desk. If this was to be his true legacy, Robert wanted to be certain that everything was arranged just so.

As he attempted to bring some order to the parchments, he was, from time to time, distracted by what was written on them. One fable, in particular, caught his eye.

> That jolly sweet season, in midst of June,
> I rose and put all sloth and sleep aside,
> And to a wood I went without a guide.

Another shout from the boys broke Robert's concentration just as he was getting started. He shuffled to his small oratory window, which overlooked a field outside the abbey walls. There he saw the boys—abbey boys, they must have been—playing at football. The day was so warm, Robert could not blame them. Had he felt strong enough, he himself would have made his way down the two flights of stairs to the outside. It was all his wasted legs could do, however, to get him from the bed to the desk or to the chamber pot. As it was, he would have to walk these summer days through woods and meadows in his writing. He returned to his fable.

> The roses red, the lily white arrayed,
> The primrose with the purple violets played;
> To hear the choirs of paradise, I say,
> Such mirth the mavis and the merle could make;
> The blossoms blithe scattered on bank and brae;
> The smell of herbs and the songbirds' cry,
> Contending who should have the victory.

Like the dreamers in the French poems, Robert's narrator received an unexpected visitor in this ideal garden, this *locus amoenus*.

> His gown was of a cloth as white as milk;
> His robe was of the finest cut and purple brown.
> His hood of scarlet, bordered well with silk;
> Fringed, it was, and to his waist hung down.

> His bonnet round, and of the old fashion;
> His beard was white, his eyes were great and gray;
> Long locks of hair upon his shoulders lay.

Robert stared into the distance of his memory to recall one of his masters of canon law at the University of Glasgow, William Arthurlie. It was Arthurlie that had taken the young Henryson into his care. Robert well remembered the awe he inspired at first, but also his passionate devotion.

> A roll of paper in his hand he bore,
> A swan's pen had he tucked above his ear,
> A gilded writing case and inkhorn fair,
> A bag of silk—all at his belt he wore.
> Thus was he goodly groomed in all his gear,
> Of stature large, and with a fearful face.
> Even where I lay he came a sturdy pace,

When stranger introduced himself as Aesop, the narrator, as might be expected, sought to be entertained by a "pretty fable." But the old man replied.

> "My son, let be,
> For what is it worth to tell a feignéd tale,
> When holy preaching may no thing avail?

> "Now in this world I think they're few or none
> Who heed God's word or give devotion;
> The ear is deaf, the heart is hard as stone;
> Now sin is blatant, without correction;
> The heart inclines to earth, looks always down.
> So cankered is the world with cancer black
> That now my tales may little succor make."

Would the telling of tales ever transform a kingdom? Even our Lord knew his parables would fall on stony ground. Was all this effort wasted? Yet Robert's Aesop had been persuaded to tell another story. For the few who heard.

Yet another shout. Robert smiled. The abbey had a more enlightened abbot now, one who realized the value of play, at intervals and in modest doses. How long had George been abbot? Some ten years or so, it must be, though the years ran together for Robert. George—the one all believed destined for greatness at court—now an abbot.

Robert left Aesop back in that dream garden. It was George he spoke with now in his memory, the fifteen-year-old who had been caught at playing the football.

"You'll know the abbot's rule."

The boy, whose gaze until this point was fixed upon some point on the flagstone, raised his head. He strove to be repentant, that Robert could see. But Robert also saw that George failed to understand why the game was so pernicious as to be banned. Rather than feign understanding, George fated himself to accept the consequences.

"Need my lord abbot know?"

Robert knew that the abbot suspected the boys of violating the rule, but till this point they had been circumspect, scheduling their games to coincide with the abbot's absence and disappearing to covert fields at the invitation of the town boys. Robert had happened upon a group of them returning from one such encounter. All scattered before he reached them, all that is but George Crichton, football in hand, and Ingram Bannatyne. Poor, loyal, foolish Ingram Bannatyne. Ingram was trembling violently; George stopped and braced himself for the storm.

Robert escorted them both to his cell, where Ingram poured forth his guilt amidst his tears. Robert could not bring himself to punish the boy further. Already Ingram had fallen into the hell of his imagination, expecting nothing less than to be burned as a notorious heretic in the market square before a crowd of jeering classmates and townsfolk. Nor did Robert attempt to extricate the names of other malefactors. Ingram was plagued by many failings. Disloyalty was not one of them. The penitent was therefore dismissed into the care of Father Charles, whose scarcely hidden amusement at the proceedings threatened to undermine Robert's authority. Robert scowled at him with a disapproval he did not feel. It was then George's turn.

"No, Abbot Henry need not know."

"And Ingram, will he be punished as well?"

"Should he be?"

"I persuaded him to join me."

"But he came of his own will?"

"Aye. I suppose he would not have been predestined."

Robert swiftly weighed the last sentence as he measured the boy's face. They had been reading the *De consolatione philosophiae*, where Boethius, the author, sought to reconcile the demands of free will, fate, and providence. George could be impudent, charmingly so, and perhaps this was the case now. Robert refused to be seduced, not only to guard his own dignity, but for the boy's own welfare. In the courts he had seen all too often the harm that could be inflicted by those accustomed to following laws of their own choosing. He was determined that it would not be so with young George Crichton.

"All the more reason to punish him, do you not think, so that he will learn not to follow bad advice and so that you will see that as a young man of privilege you have a responsibility for others beyond yourself?"

"He suffers greatly already and will suffer more to see me punished alone. I pray you to show mercy on him."

"And will you yourself be merciful when you have occasion, as occasion you certainly will have?"

"Aye, Master Robert."

"Then so be it. I will not punish Ingram."

"Thank you, sir."

"As for you, I will remit the customary strokes of the birch. Instead, you will translate portions of Cicero's *De officiis*. In this way, I trust you will come to apprehend the responsibilities laid before you. You may go."

George bowed his head. Just as he made for the door, he turned around. "Begging your pardon, sir, do you believe the abbot's rule to be just?"

Robert admired the boy's pluck but had to play his role yet. "That's an impertinent question. My personal feelings are of little concern. The order of the school and the abbey is to be maintained."

The barest wisp of a smile and a nod told Robert that George was learning to play another kind of game.

George was a ward of the great border lord, William, Third Lord Crichton, but beyond this his background was a mystery. Rumor whispered that he was a member of a cadet branch of the family that had suffered some misfortune and left the child in the care of a powerful, rich, and—fortunately—benevolent relative. Whatever his origins, George, of all the boys, had his future ensured. His schooling was a formality, a token gesture on the Lord Crichton's part to abide by the spirit of the new age—that sons of the nobility be educated so as to serve crown and country more perfectly and with greater polish. In two years, at the age of sixteen, George would enter service, either in Crichton's court or in the king's. There he would fulfill his apprenticeship of sorts. Were he to distinguish himself sufficiently, the king might appoint him a knight of the realm, a counselor, a lord of parliament; there might even be a lordship or earldom in the future. For all of this no university degree was required.

The abbot had no intention of conspiring in the young Crichton's success by turning a blind eye and deaf ear to his trespasses. Football was symptomatic of moral and spiritual laxity that infected the whole kingdom. The removal of the game might not, by itself, knit together the torn moral fabric. Abbot Henry did, however, believe in the power of symbolic action. For his part, Robert believed that one might have too many symbols, like too many possessions. They might begin to clutter the imagination, drawing attention to themselves, thus hiding that which they were meant to reveal. He thus settled on discipline, not punishment. The distinction might be a fine one, but he was determined to maintain it.

The next afternoon, George appeared in the scriptorium, where Robert had the manuscript of *De officiis* opened at one of the writing desks. He designated the passages to be translated and then sat down nearby. He observed a scowl break out on the boy's face as the size of the task became apparent. Perhaps this was not so merciful a reprieve. A birching might be preferable—painful, but soon over. For five afternoons George labored, then submitted his work for Robert's inspection. Robert skimmed through the translation and smiled.

> ...*hominis est propria veri inquisitio atque investigatio.*
> ...the man who is a true man digs for truth.
> ...*nemini parere animus bene informatus a natura velit nisi praecipienti aut docenti aut utilitatis causa iuste et legitime imperanti;*
> ...a mind well-crafted by Nature will not abide just any command, only ones given by wise teachers and just lords who rule for the sake of the common good.
> ...*ex quo magnitudo animi existit humanarumque rerum contemptio.*
> Such a man gains greatness of spirit and counts all things worldly not worth a fly.

"You've taken some liberty with Cicero's letter, but I grant you've caught his spirit. Now let me see how much you remember."

A shadow eclipsed George's face.

For the next hour, Robert quizzed his prisoner and also instructed him on the essence of Cicero's thought. There was little new the boy would discover, but Robert keenly desired to sum up all that Master Cuthbert before him had tried to instill.

"What are Plato's rules?"

"That in everything he does, the lord will keep the good of all the people in fixed view, whatever his own interests are; and that he will not allow the interests of any one party to undermine the common good."

"Aye. And what is 'decorum'?"

"It is living consistently, both in our entire lives and in our separate actions. We must, however, not neglect the gifts God has bestowed on us in trying to acquire the ones he's given to others."

"Very good. And the '*miles gloriosus*'?"

George smiled. "The braggart knight."

Robert quizzed George further: on the virtues and their corruption; on the proper relationship between Reason and appetite; on the role of Nature, then Fortune in shaping a man's calling; on the claims of the country on one's loyalty; on public service as a sacred trust; on the proper way to respond to abuse by one's enemies, with dignity and calm.

"Well, be off with you." The schoolmaster waved his arm when his interrogation was finished.

"Thank you, sir."

Robert's dismissal was accompanied by a silent prayer that George would find the will to bend his gifts toward the common good, of his fellow choristers now and of his fellow countrymen later.

Robert could not protect George forever. The cruel irony was that the next time George ran afoul of the abbot's rule, it was not his fault. Nor, in truth, had he broken that rule at all. It happened that on an early spring Saturday afternoon, when the weather was unseasonably warm, George organized a wapenshaw among the older choristers, some twenty-five boys ranging in age from fourteen to sixteen. Turning out with weapons for instruction, practice, and display was considered a more manly way to exhibit one's prowess than by frivolous sport. Such was the opinion of Parliament, which frequently encouraged, indeed commanded, the practice as a means keeping the citizenry fit for warfare.

George organized the party into two opposing ranks. The majority, since they were the sons of tradesmen or merchants, were pikemen, armed with crude staves. He and one or two others had wooden swords and shields, more befitting their rank in society. John had been coerced to come along, assured that this activity was licit. George appointed him chaplain, though he was given a sword also. A fighting priest was held in great esteem. And to Ingram, whose clumsiness posed as much a danger to his friends as to his enemies, was honored as standard bearer. Bows were laid aside for archery practice later.

The two sides began a mock encounter, thrusting and parrying according to the rule of arms described by George, but in slow motion so as not to hurt one another. It was then that the warm weather and Fate drew the town boys to the same field. Ordinarily, they would have been welcomed by cheers, but today was different. Military exercises were much more absorbing than childish play.

When the town boys could not coax the choristers to play, they began mocking them. Although chafed by the taunts, George underwent one of those moments in life where maturity comes not in a trickle, but in a torrent. He determined to hold his warriors together. Were this real combat and were his troops to be distracted and disorganized, the battle would be lost and they would be destroyed. His own reading and the stories he had heard from his guardian told him that much. King Harold had lost England to William the Bastard for just such a reason.

Inspired by George's example, both troops from the abbey maintained their order despite a rain of abuse. Soon, however, that rain took on a material form. The town boys raided the bows and arrows left unguarded by the side of the field and began to shoot at the combatants. The ends of the shafts were blunted, but their force could inflict pain enough. There were also enough arrows that the bombardment would not end soon. George decided that a surprise attack would force the invaders to drop their weapons and flee the field. In this he miscalculated. He should have known from past football matches that these apprentice tanners, shoemakers, blacksmiths, and the like were the future yeomen of Scotland's armies. Brawling was their meat and drink.

Mother Scotland would have been proud of her sons that day. George gave the command to wheel about, and his fellow "earl" among the choristers readily took up the role of lieutenant, master of the left flank. The boys behind them joined ranks and charged. Despite his weight, Ingram managed to stick by George's side. Even John got caught up in the moment and, if for no other reason than to protect Ingram, loped along beside his friend.

There was sufficient time for only one more flight of arrows before the inevitable clash, but that was enough. Ingram yelped in pain and pawed at his left eye, where an arrow had struck him a glancing blow. He slowed for a moment and the standard wavered. For the briefest of seconds, George wavered, also, uncertain whether to move forward or to attend to his wounded standard bearer. The whole line slowed. Others had been hit by the arrows, though none as seriously as Ingram. The pain had, however, shocked them. John pulled at Ingram's arm to lead him from the field. By now, blood seeped through Ingram's hand and trickled down his face into the corner of his mouth. He stabbed at it with his tongue, then spit it out. Suddenly, he gave what was meant to be a roar. It was more like a cat's screech, but there was no mistaking his intent. He shook off John's grasp and resumed his charge, his left hand still covering his damaged eye. Even George was hard-pressed to keep up with him.

All this lasted only seconds, less time than it later took John to chronicle the event to Robert. The apprentices thus had no time to reload their weapons before the onslaught, so they used the bows to defend themselves. They were driven back a few yards, but their own line did not wilt. They were not about to be defeated by mere song birds, although in truth the lineage of most on both sides was similar.

To hear John describe the meeting, nothing in the annals of warfare could match the concussion of those two armies—fist against chin, stave against head, wooden sword against rib. The youth of the combatants in no way diminished the glory of that encounter. The battle another Stirling Bridge, George another William Wallace. Robert suspected that the recent appearance of Blind Hary's Wallace book, which was fueling Scottish passions against the English and which had made its way into the abbey library, was coloring John's narrative.

"George was magnificent, everywhere at once, shouting orders, encouraging his troops."

"And Ingram?"

"He fought like an enraged bear at the stake. None of the townsfolk could come within the standard's length of him—he swept it around like a great scythe."

The sound of horns warned the combatants that the burgh constables had been notified. Although the provost and aldermen were keen to maintain order, the constables themselves operated on the principle that a little "blood-letting" among the young was a healthy thing. The horns were an intentional warning. Any boy foolish enough to be caught deserved his punishment.

Abbot Henry was less understanding. No amount of coloring on John's part would make his lord abbot see the matter in anything but black and white. This was nothing more than a brawl, to be expected of ordinary folk, but not his boys. When he heard the horns, he rode immediately with Prior Gerald to the scene. Robert and Brother Martin followed on mules. They were met along the way by the constables and their deputies, who were forced to pick up their desultory pace to keep abreast of the fiery abbot.

When they arrived, there was little to see. Everyone—chorister and apprentice alike—had vanished, and with them all weapons and evidence of battle. Only George remained. He stood alone, head bowed, waiting for the inquisition that was certain to follow.

It was said that Abbot Henry saw only in black and white. That is not quite true. When his gaze swept the field, there lay a football, long abandoned, long forgotten. This, he concluded, was the source of all the iniquity. His limited palette now included red.

George stood up to face the wrath. "My lord abbot—"

"Lord me no lords, young man. If you name me lord, then obey me as one. My ruling on the playing of football was clear, was it not?"

"Aye, my lord."

"But you played anyway?"

"Nay, my lord."

"And that, I suppose, is a breviary by which you were leading the other lads in their devotions?" Abbot Henry pointed toward the offending object. His voice held no trace of humor.

George said nothing. His gaze was undefiant, but steady. His coolness only enraged the abbot.

"O, so you are the rat that would bell the cat? Give the other mice a chance to run? No, indeed, my young sir. The mice shall be smoked from their hiding places. They, not you, shall pay the penalty of disobedience. Then we shall see how willing they are to follow my lord rat in the future."

"I beg you, my lord—" This had not gone as George planned, and he made to kneel. But the abbot turned his palfrey and galloped off, scowling at the constables as he passed them. Prior Gerald followed, then the constables, who shrugged at one another and grinned. George looked up at Robert in silence, but with pleading in his eyes. Robert jerked his head as a sign for George to mount behind him, and together they rode with Brother Martin back to the abbey.

"We were not playing ball." The tone was not defensive. "It was a wapenshaw we were having. The others wanted us to play, but we would not join them. It was then that they attacked us."

"Who won?" Brother Martin surprised the other two by his question. All his life he had endured taunts as to his manliness, for his vocation both as monk and as musician. He, too, had a stake in the matter. "Who won?" he repeated. The surprise took a moment to wear off.

"The horns halted the affray, but we still held our line."

Martin nodded, then smiled in his gentle, beatific way.

"Is there something you can do?" George asked Robert.

"The abbot is angry, certain enough. We best let him cool. I will do what I can."

When they arrived, however, the abbot was even more irate. Ingram's injury was serious. The anesthetic of his wrath had worn off and he had groaned all the way back through the woods, nursed all the while by John. Brother Kenneth, the infirmarian, had had to pry the two apart. John was now congregated with the other choristers before the abbot's house in plain view of the townsfolk, who had gathered to watch events unfold. When Robert saw this, he whispered to George to dismount. Better that the abbot not see him riding into the burgh, even if on a mule.

Judgment was summary, punishment swift. It was George who had to wield the cane, with the threat that if he did not strike hard enough, Nicholas, the burgh blacksmith and father of one of the boys who had instigated the fight, would be only too eager to oblige. To humiliate the boys even further, the abbot forced them to hike their gowns up to their buttocks. George was commanded to strike their thighs. Although he attempted to pull his strokes, the pain he inflicted was real enough.

"Let's see what a leader you are," the abbot said to George when the spectacle was over. "It's one thing to command men if they follow you to places where they want to go. But if they follow you now—" he paused to survey the line of boys struggling not to rub their legs—"then you can call yourself a leader." He turned back to George and stared at him. George held the abbot's gaze. He said nothing but gripped the cane tightly.

"You'd be using that on me, like as not." The abbot descended from his mount. "Then come, boy. You have my permission. You'll not suffer any consequences if you overcome me. And if I overcome you, your shame will be consequence enough." He stood face to face with George. Robert looked at them both. The "boy" was nearly as tall as the abbot and to see them face to face was like looking at an object and its image in a mirror. Neither wavered in his stance, both worked their jaws behind tightly pressed lips, neither blinked. The few seconds they stood this way seemed interminable. Then George did an unexpected thing. He smiled. The same charming smile Robert had seen so often. George knelt and handed the cane up to the abbot, horizontally, as if offering fealty. The abbot was furious. He took the cane and brought it down with all his might on George's shoulder. George winced, but rose and joined the other boys. The abbot turned about and staggered to his house. Prior Gerald followed him.

The crowd from the burgh drifted away by twos and threes. When it had all but vanished, Brother Martin said to the boys, "All right, my lads, let's tend to your wounds."

A few of the boys made to follow him. George spoke. His voice was quiet, but firm. "With all due respect, sir, the abbot has not dismissed us."

"Aye, but certainly he means for you to go now."

"No doubt, but until he gives express command—" Those who had moved turned to one another, then bowed to their choirmaster and rejoined the others.

Martin looked to Robert for help. The schoolmaster simply shrugged. He, too, was convinced that the abbot's departure had been a dismissal, but he also knew that the abbot's foul humor might be hunting for excuses to punish the boys further. At the same time, the abbot had folded in public and was not likely to appear in public for a while. The boys might have a long wait.

So they remained throughout the rest of the afternoon, sore and, in some cases, bleeding. One or two collapsed from exhaustion. Several relieved themselves in their clothing. Robert and Martin remained with them and moved about in their midst to tend to those in most desperate need. In defiance of abbey rules, Father Charles brought a flask of wine from the cellar and urged the boys to drink. All except George did. He remained standing, eyes fixed, that enigmatic smile lingering on his face. Only by the greatest self-restraint did Robert avoid glancing at the upstairs window of the abbot's house. He feared what he might see—demonic rage, glutted satisfaction, or impotent remorse. Perhaps he feared something even worse—casual neglect that had fixed itself on a more pressing object.

Towards evening, the door of the abbot's house opened, and Prior Gerald emerged. He spoke. "Abbot Crichton bids me to dismiss you to prepare for vespers."

An appearance by the abbot himself would have signaled a complete victory, but Robert knew that this would never happen. He prayed that George would realize the same and that the young man would allow the abbot a means by which to save face. His prayers were answered. George bowed to Prior Gerald. "Please convey to our lord abbot our thanks and our intention to serve God and him in all things." The boys hobbled off to their dormitory.

From that day on, little on the surface seemed different. True, the boys' loyalty to George only deepened. They did not hold their punishment against him. The escapade had bestowed on each a badge of honor, unseen, but nonetheless real. Soon, however, they fell back into their old ways. Their heroic exertions on the battlefield carried little momentum, especially in their classes. They performed most unheroically in their classwork, with none of the concentration that won them glory elsewhere. They had returned to being simply boys.

But Robert knew that everything for George had changed. He organized no more clandestine wapenshaws or football games. He devoted to his studies a kind of intensity that amounted almost to desperation. He had much lost time to make up, and the results did not improve dramatically, but improve they did. And he visited Ingram in the infirmary every afternoon during that boy's recovery. Brother Kenneth, despite his greatest efforts, was unable to recover Ingram's sight in the wounded eye. The boy was destined to wear a patch for the rest of his days. While he lay swathed in bandages, George and John set about to reading to him Blind Hary's epic poem about the Wallace. By the end of the week, when all but the patch had been removed, this had become such a ritual that they continued to read, even when Ingram could manage for himself.

To the abbot, George was respectful and distantly courteous. He bowed at their occasional meetings and spoke when he was spoken to; otherwise, he made no attempts to ingratiate himself. At the end of the school year, he received a summons from Lord Crichton to return to Crichton castle. His life as a courtier had begun.

These reveries vanished in the light wind stirring through the open window. Robert took one last look at the boys before returning to his desk. There he continued reading the fable he had begun, of a lion who went to sleep and woke to find mice dancing on his stomach and beard. In outrage, the king of beasts grabbed the leader of the mice and demanded:

> "Knew thou not well I was both lord and king
> Of creatures all?" "Yes," said the mouse, "I know,

But I misknew, because ye lay so low."

"Thy false excuse," the lion said again,
"Shall not avail one mite, I undertake.
I put the case: had I been dead or slain,
And then my carcass been stuffed full of straw,
Though thou had found my figure lying so,
Because it bore the print of my person,
Thou should for fear on knees have fallen down."

Was a king who did not act like a king still a king? This conundrum had vexed minds greater than Robert's. Unhappily, it refused to remain the property of schoolmen. On that afternoon George had found that the same question might be asked as well of an abbot; and some six years later, in 1482, it was to loom before all three boys—Ingram, John, and George—with fatal consequences.

In the little mouse's case, the king, whether he acted as king or not, still held the power.

"For thy trespass thou can make no defence;
Therefore, thou suffer shall one shameful end
And death, such as to treason is decreed,
Onto the gallows high hanged by the feet."

Robert envisioned the poor mouse pleading for his life, marshalling reasons why the angry lion should not carry out his doom.

"In every judge's heart should mercy be
As assessours and collateral;
Without mercy, justice is cruelty,
As said is in the laws spiritual.
When rigor sits upon the tribunal,
The equity of law who may sustain?
Few or none, except mercy goes between."

The mouse concluded that even such lowly creatures as he might have some part to play in a king's affairs.

Moved by his subject's contrition, the lion laid aside his anger and showed compassion. Soon, however, he found himself in bondage, trapped by rural folk whose lands he had terrorized. The mouse, whom he had set free, heard his cries and beckoned to his fellows:

> "Unless we help him, succour knows he none.
> Come help requite one good turn for another;
> Go, loose him soon"; and they said, "yea, good brother."

> They took no knife, their teeth were sharp enough;
> To see that sight, forsooth, it was great wonder—
> How that they ran among the ropes so tough,
> Before, behind, some went above, some under,
> And gnawed the ropes and tore the net asunder;
> Then bade him rise, and he uprose anon,
> And thanked them all; then on his way is gone.

To each of the main actors in the story, Robert's Aesop had assigned allegorical parts to play. The mighty lion, of course, signified a king, who, though he should diligently govern his people, took

> no labor
> To rule and steer the land and justice keep,
> But lies all still in lusts and sloth and sleep.

The mice were the common folk, who will ignore the law and will rebel against lawful authority if their rulers give them no guidance. The rural folk

> that woven have the net
> In which the lion suddenly was taken,
> Waited patiently amends to get,
> For injured men write in the marble stone.

But events in 1482 had rendered more precise interpretation unnecessary. Aesop acknowledged as much.

> More to expound, for now, I let alone,
> But king and lord may well know what I mean:
> Figure hereof in our time has been seen.

In Aesop's voice, Robert concluded the *moralitas* with a plea,

> "That treason of this country be exiled,
> And justice reign, and lords ay keep their faith
> Unto their sovereign king both night and day."

Such had been the benediction that William Arthurlie had pronounced after examining Robert for the licentiate in the laws, and it had been Robert's prayer for these past twenty-some years. It was the prayer that even now he spent his precious breath praying.

IX

Orpheus and Eurydice

After reading the "Lion and the Mouse," Robert placed it in the collection of his fables. He bound the leaves with a ribbon and laid it together with three other stacks, bound in like manner—his "Cresseid," an assortment of minor poems, and a third he called "Orpheus and Eurydice." This last packet he untied and withdrew three letters hidden under the last leaf. As he did so, he heard a soft scratching at the door. At first he thought it must be Charles with his dinner. The latch, however, did not move. Instead, Robert saw a white paw flailing hopefully under the cell door. It was the cat, Augustina, so named because her black and white markings resembled the habit of the Augustinian canons. She was the only cat allowed to roam the dormitory freely as mousecatcher. She must have smelled Robert's guests. A deep-throated yowl issued from out in the hallway.

"Whsst, be off with you. You'll not be disturbing my wee family this night." Robert threw a mug of water under the door. The yowl turned into a screech, and the paw disappeared.

He began to survey the letters. Together, they chronicled his life during those those months from December of 1481 until the following August. The first opened with these words: "From Margaret, Queen of Scotland, Princess of Denmark, to Master Robert Henryson, greetings in the name

of our Lord Jesu Christ...." Although disappointed that he had never received another invitation to read at court, he still had the queen's letter,
which conjured up the memory of torchlight reflected in her tears on that
December evening so many years before.

The second letter had come the following March. Written in an accom-
plished secretary hand, it could mean a letter from court. Another invitation to read, perhaps? But the seal, though vaguely familiar, was not the
royal insignia. He remembered breaking the wax with some agitation:

> To the most venerable Master Robert Henryson, greetings.
>
> It seemed fitting to send my poor congratulations on your Cresseid
> book. Having heard, on good report, that you read it before their
> royal majesties, I obtained a copy, through no small effort, and
> read it with much interest and emotion. I have ever admired your
> poetry and put little stock in the opinion of this world. Still, it is
> delightful to have one's opinions confirmed by the esteem and af-
> fection of others whose tastes are unassailable. Rumor has named
> you our nation's Chaucer. I concur.
> Lest you deem me an indiscriminate flatterer, I pose this one ques-
> tion: is the misfortunate Cresseid to find no peace?
>
> Ever your most humble and obedient pupil,
> Isabel Inglis

Agitation from another source shook his hands as he read. Visions of
the young Isabel and of Father Ninian's gnarled finger pointed in warning rose simultaneously before him. He composed himself and re-read
the letter. The passage of many years had long since cooled any ardor he
might have felt for the girl. Nor did it appear that hers for him lingered,
either. The tone of the letter was innocent enough. He bid Ninian's finger
farewell.

Trying to find Isabel proved to be no small feat. She had signed her
maiden name; but like many matrons he knew in his experience as a notary, she may have done so to maintain a clear right to any inheritance
from her father. Certainly, there must be a husband and bairns. He sought
out the deliverer of the letter, one Brother Benedict, who served as courier
between Dunfermline and its neighboring monasteries. But other pressing correspondence from Abbot Henry had sped the messenger on to In-

verkeithing.

A week later had found Robert en route to Edinburgh in the company of the abbey librarian, Brother Dominic, who was delivering the illuminated book of hours and psalter to Isaac Abercrombie, Bookseller. The scriptorium at Dunfermline had achieved a reputation for producing manuscripts of high quality at a price just within the range of a merchant conscious of improving his social standing by the library that ornamented his house. Abercrombie had commissioned the manuscripts on behalf of one of the prominent families in the royal city. The illustrations were few, but adequately rendered. Purchasing books for the grammar school with the endowment provided by Richard de Leith gave Robert an excuse for the journey, though his reason lay elsewhere.

Dominic, who had been librarian at the abbey for as long as Robert had been alive, housed a library in his own mind. He could name the provenance and describe the history of every book in his charge. He could recount the biographies of previous owners. He knew watermarks, scribal hands. It was safe to say that he knew intimately the handwriting of some hundreds of pages in the library because it had been his hand that had produced them. He had traveled to libraries as far as Germany and was on familiar terms with the papal librarian in the Vatican.

Dominic guarded the library with all the zeal of the keeper of the royal treasure, but within its precincts, he operated with an almost prodigal generosity. The books were his friends by long hours of communion with them, and he wished to acquaint others with them. It pained him deeply that the younger monks and the schoolboys frequently looked upon them as the collection of mere words.

There was no tap to Dominic's conversation. It flowed, at times gushed, with little pause. Charles had warned Robert that no visit to the library could ever be brief when the old man was on duty. But this talkativeness was not the product of old age. Dominic would meander from topic to topic, but always returned to the point he had begun, however far away he had wandered. One could hardly be angry—each discourse was filled with a rare erudition, but one had to plan encounters carefully.

The one-day trip to Edinburgh, by reason of Dominic's advanced age, took two. Dominic filled the time with animated talk on Lorenzo Valla's *De elegantia linguae latinae*, a cornerstone of the new learning. It was this book, which had come to his attention during a stay in Rome several years previously, that he would buy with the proceeds from the sale of the psalter and book of hours. Abercrombie not only bought books, his scribes produced inexpensive copies to sell.

Once at the bookseller's, after courtesies had been exchanged, Robert knew that he had the better part of the day to himself. Dominic and old Abercrombie would be at their trading for some hours, each sharpening the other's hunger for books they had seen or procured. Invariably, Dominic brought back more manuscripts than he had come for. The chief comfort that the abbot took from these unauthorized purchases was that Dominic also received lucrative commissions, which offset the expenses. Robert set off toward the Cowgate, where he had last lived with the Inglis family.

His hopes of finding Isabel quickly turned bitter almost from the start. The intervening years had severed almost completely the fragile threads that bound him to his former life. Old age had escorted Father Ninian to the grave. That much he already knew. But others had departed as well. Alexander Inglis had died unexpectedly not long after Robert had left. The plague had also taken Malcolm Inglis, the older of the two sons.

Samuel lacked the mental agility and determination of his older brother, and without his aid soon lost the family's license to export wool to Middleburgh in the Low Countries and to import its finished cloth. His only salvation had literally come from Mother Church, in the person of Sarah Ogilvie, the widowed sister of the priest of the parish church where the Inglis family had worshiped. Alexander, before his death, had endowed a chapel in the church in honor of Lazarus, the patron saint of lepers and outcasts. From the very first time he heard the story of Dives and Lazarus, Alexander had been tormented with the fear that he too would suffer in the afterlife for his wealth in the present. The beggars in the neighborhood could expect a coin from him, but the size varied in proportion to how much his conscience ached at the moment.

While helping his father make the arrangements for the chapel, Samuel met Sarah, whose husband, John Gilchrist, had recently died. A short time later, when tragedy struck the Inglis household, Samuel and Sarah married. She was some ten years his senior. She kept her brother's house and Samuel oversaw the church grounds and livestock. It was just as much responsibility, under the watchful eye of Father Iain, Sarah's brother, as he was fitted for; and the life agreed with him. "Like the cunning steward in the Gospels"—Samuel described his position to Robert with a sly wink—"only not quite so dishonest."

Robert laughed. The man was guileless to the point of simplicity and had always shown the sweetest temper of the three children. Only when Robert mentioned Isabel's name did the tenor of the conversation change.

"Hush, man. Her name'll not be mentioned in this house."

Robert was taken aback by the force of Samuel's response, but persisted. "She wrote me this letter, and I'll be trying to find her."

Samuel would not even glance at the extended parchment. Sarah, drawn by her husband's anger, had appeared silently in the doorway and stood behind him. By nature a timid woman, who had been raised in the dark, authoritarian shadow of her brother, she twisted her fingers nervously. Robert detected a quick motion of her eyes toward the church. With a barely perceptible nod, he shifted to the safer topic of the garden. Samuel, eager to leave the painful topic of his sister, softened. His anger at Isabel was obviously too great a burden to be carried for very long. With a sigh he spoke of manured soil that in his mind had already yielded beans and kale and turnips. Even at this stage, the carefully shaped beds, the evenly spaced rows, the neatly trimmed margins all spoke more eloquently of Samuel's true gifts than ever commerce had done.

After a polite interval, Robert excused himself, citing as his reason a desire to offer prayer for the souls of Samuel's brother and father in the Inglis chapel. April had done little to drive off the damp winter chill inside the small church. Robert pulled his cloak about him as he knelt to pray. Or tried to pray. Samuel's words had greatly troubled him and now cast over Isabel's letter an ominous shadow. He could only guess at the enormity of her sin that had created such a wound in the family, a wound that now festered in an ever-hardening shell of silence. His reflections had barely focused themselves into prayer before he felt a slight tap on his shoulder. He looked up to see Sarah.

"Begging your pardon, Master Robert. If you'll follow me."

Robert stood and Sarah led him to a corner of the choir, where they would not be observed by anyone who happened into the nave.

"My brother's visiting old Megan Carmichael, who's dying, and Samuel will be driving the cattle to the next field."

"You wanted to speak to me?"

"Aye. I could not help but overhear."

"I'm trying to find Isabel, his sister. She wrote me."

"Samuel's that angry with her and has been these twenty years. I am not certain he even knows where she is."

"Twenty years?" Robert exclaimed. "What did she do?"

"All of this happened well before we were married. Samuel would speak of it but little, enough to blame her for sending his poor father to his grave.

And Malcolm's death he called a judgment on the family for aiding in her wickedness."

"In Jesu's name, tell me what she did."

"Samuel's father was eager that Isabel marry well and so introduced her to the Lord Crichton's third son, Edward."

"Aye, that I know. I was with them at the betrothal feast at Crichton Castle."

"Not long after you left the family, it would seem, the young man was killed while hunting. Soon thereafter, Isabel was discovered to be with child. No one doubted who the father was, but she never named Edward specifically. As a result, Lord Crichton refused to acknowledge the poor girl. It was grief, not age, that killed her father. Malcolm would have let her return, but died from the plague within a month of his father. Samuel would have nothing to do with her after that."

"Where did she go?"

"The Poor Clares here in Edinburgh took her in. They pleaded with Samuel to take Isabel into his home after the child was born. Samuel refused and has closed the door to his sister ever since. The bairn never survived."

"And your brother told you all this?"

"Aye. He can be a hard man, Iain, but good, and he saw no reason to prevent Samuel from taking my hand because of the sins of his family."

As Robert studied the aging, homely face of this woman, he suspected that brother Iain was shrewd, if nothing else, and had accepted the best offer he could get for his sister before the market closed altogether. Were he so good, why had he not brought the poor Isabel within the kingdom of his kindness, even if to feed her on the scraps from under his table?

"I must go." Sarah gestured nervously. "My brother and husband will be wanting their dinner soon. Will you be joining us?"

Robert shook his head. "I must be on my way. One of the abbey brothers will be expecting me. I'll be at my prayers for the family and then off."

He extended his hand by way of parting. Sarah took it and clung to it at first as if in desperation. Then, realizing her presumption, she dropped it quickly, darting glances about the church all the while.

"May you find her well."

"Aye, and may Jesu protect you."

For the first time, Sarah smiled. The homeliness nearly disappeared.

"And you, good Master."

On the way back to the bookseller's on the Royal Mile, Robert made a detour to the Greyfriars' abbey, to which was attached the convent and hospital. He was escorted to Mother Anne, the prioress.

"You'll have little to show for your pains, Master Robert Henryson," Mother Anne said, upon being informed of the object of Robert's quest. "We have not seen Isabel these twenty years."

"My journey'll not be wasted if I might find out anything about her."

"What is it you'll be asking? We're not in the habit of resurrecting the miseries of God's poor creatures."

"My curiosity is not an idle one. She was a pupil of mine before she came your way, when I was tutor for her brothers. An apt lass, she was."

Mother Anne was silent.

"I was not the father, if that's what you'll be thinking."

"It's not my business to speculate."

"I have not seen the family since, but she sent me this letter. I'd be grateful for your aid in finding her."

The Mother read the letter and sat thoughtfully for a time before she answered. "The Lord blessed us with memory to preserve the lives of those we hold dear. Do not bring misery to her and to yourself, but hold her dear as you remember her."

"And is her crime so great as all that, that I should abandon her?"

"Did she ask to see you?" The soft voice had an iron rod running through it.

Robert knew that she hadn't and stuttered a feeble, "Neither did she not ask."

"But she gave you no place of abode."

"Then tell me where she is. What harm can there be? I cannot desert her if she is in need. Her family have done that already."

"And can you not leave her to God?"

"God gifted us with memory to remind us of our duty. Perhaps God will not have her left to himself alone."

"Then I will write to her. If she agrees, I will tell you where she abides. Or she will write you herself."

Mother Anne put forth her hand, and Robert kissed it. "Jesu bless you."

Anne signed the cross of benediction and gently laid her hand on his head. "Be blessed and be wise."

The journeys to and from Edinburgh closely resembled one another, with the exception that now Brother Dominic was able to show Robert the manuscripts he had earlier described. Robert strove to maintain a veneer of interest, but his mind was on Isabel. He prayed that she would write, that she would not simply disappear from his life again, as she had done so many years before. Even if she did not reveal her whereabouts, he welcomed her correspondence.

A month later his prayer was answered. Brother Benedict delivered to him another letter.

To the most venerable Master Robert Henryson, greetings.

Mother Anne has informed me of your desire that we might meet. Nothing would give me greater pleasure. Please hold no grudge against her for keeping my whereabouts secret. She merely wished to spare us both pain. You will find that I am much changed from the child who sat at my father's board while you instructed Malcolm and Samuel. What remains unchanged is that child's affection for her schoolmaster.

You will find me at the Spital House of St. Luke the Physician, just outside the walls of Stirling.

Go with God.

Your obedient servant, Isabel Inglis

So this was why Mother Anne had urged him not to pursue this course? Perhaps she did not think him strong enough to see the conditions of Isabel's penance and her ministry. He would show that he was made of sterner matter. He would visit the leper hospital the following Saturday.

So it was that two days later found him on his mule, picking his way through the crowded burgh of Dunfermline. As he left the northern gate and entered the King's Highway to Stirling, he left behind the sweet blue gauze of woodsmoke, the cries of vendors peddling tin pots and freshly slaughtered chickens, and the clashing aromas of raw meat, stale sweat, piss, meat pies, and beer. He much preferred the silence and the savors of spring that greeted him in the countryside.

The leper house was but a half mile east of Stirling, near where he had seen the leper band that December. It might have been ten miles, or a hundred, for that matter. No one but the Franciscan sisters who ministered to the sick and a few compassionate relatives of the victims ever ventured that way. Revulsion at this decayed humanity was only one reason. Fear of being infected with the disease was a second. The third—the moral taint—was perhaps the most compelling. Such a terrible punishment must follow an equally terrible sin. Most folk suspected that lepers had gone the way of Robert's Cresseid, that their promiscuity had stirred the Almighty to such extremes.

A wall surrounded the hospital and Robert pulled the bell rope to signal his arrival. One of the sisters led him to a chamber, where a fire fought off the chill of the winter and the stone. A small opening in one wall gave view to an adjoining room.

"She'll be expecting you," the sister murmured before closing the door behind him. Before long, he heard a shuffling in the next room, and a stooped figure appeared at the opening. Although the white wrappings on the hands appeared to be clean, stains from the oozing sores were already beginning to grow.

The figure stopped and straightened as much as it could. Its face displayed all the customary marks of the disease: the decaying nose and lips, the welts. It then spoke. The voice was raspy, but there was no mistaking it, even after all these years.

"Good day, Master Robert."

For a moment Robert stood paralyzed. His legs then found life and, without a word, he rushed out the spital door and through the gate. Kneeling by the roadside, he relieved himself of his breakfast in a ditch. He stared at his vomitus in fascination, like a soldier, stunned by the blow that has mortally wounded him, who grasps with his eye the last detail, however minute, of the life he is about to leave.

A pair of Franciscan brothers were just turning into the gate. One put his arm around Robert as he leaned over. "Are you all right, man?" the friar asked. "Might I help you?" Robert was too ashamed even to answer. He shook his head, then mounted his mule to begin the journey back to Dunfermline. He dared not even look back at the friars.

Throughout the journey, Robert's mind focused on a single picture— the diseased Isabel—but the picture refused to remain static. It grew in his imagination so that as the day wore on it became an even greater monstrosity. He brushed by the abbey porter, ignoring the customary greeting, and rushed to his cell. There he wept.

For the whole of the next week, Robert wrestled with God and with his own spirit. Revulsion, disappointment, anger, compassion, jealousy. Each emotion warred for dominance, each doubling back after it had been displaced by the others. The intimacy with the young Crichton he could understand, even if he had trouble forgiving. Crichton and Isabel were betrothed. And the child? An unfortunate consequence of an unhappy affair. At least God had been merciful. The bairn had not lived to enter the world fatherless and branded as a bastard. But the leprosy? How many others had there been since Crichton? Had the judgment he imagined for Cresseid been laid upon the one woman he had ever felt such affection for?

Tormented night after sleepless night, Robert grew impatient with his boys and swung his rod on their hands and legs with fury and frequency. He decided to seek the advice of Father Charles. Over the years, Robert had seen the wisdom of the abbot's decision of yoking him with this jolly confessor, whose God would be more amused (or annoyed) than offended by his penitent's dyspeptic confessions. Robert envied this man, who one moment might regale his audience with stories of piss and farts (the latter, by way of accompaniment, he was able to produce on demand by some miraculous ability), and the next, during divine service, weep at the great suffering of our Savior for his sins. Perhaps Charles could help him see a clear way in all this. They arranged to meet in the chapter house after the abbey business had been concluded for that morning.

"And what has been pricking your conscience today, Master Robert?" Charles began. "Fear that you have not been working your students hard enough? Too much time at prayers and not enough in your studies?"

All Robert could manage was a sigh.

"It's serious, then, is it? You can tell me, my old friend."

Robert needed no coaxing and began pouring out his story. It was the first time he had admitted to himself how deeply he affected his former pupil and how much he had felt betrayed by her. When he finished, Father Charles was silent. The laughter had disappeared from his eyes. Robert felt justified in his concern.

"It's penance you'll be wanting, Robert, not advice."

Robert drew back.

"O aye. The woman'll not need your judgment. Someone has laid upon her his own, and I'm not so sure it'll be the Lord."

"What would you be having me do?"

"Go back to her. Do not leave her alone in her distress. It's a leper Abraham held in his own bosom and a leper that St. Francis kissed. I'm thinking you'll be in good company. Hardly a penance; more of an honor you'll not be deserving." At this Father Charles smiled. "Whatever she may have done to bring this on herself—and I've my doubts as to the cause of this dread ill—it's the truth that no man'll be having her now. She'll be all your own. Now I've got my casks to be tending."

Father Charles made to go but patted Robert on the shoulder. "You said you once fancied the lass. Give fancy a true pair of eyes to see by." He paused. "A poet's eyes."

For the rest of that day, Robert skulked about the abbey like one stricken himself by the dread disease, as if Father Charles had exposed the oozing sores of his heart to the brothers. Imagining their communal judgment on him, he averted his eyes whenever he met one in the corridors. As a layperson, he was not required to attend divine service; and though certain that he would be missed, he absented himself from sext, nones, vespers, and compline. He also fasted through the midday and evening meals.

That night Robert slept but fitfully. Isabel's face haunted him. He saw in her bleared eyes no judgment…only the pain of betrayal—his own. During one of several brief spells of sleep, he dreamed of the story of Orpheus, the legendary Greek musician, and his queen, Eurydice, only it was he and Isabel, both in their younger days, that his imagination saw. It was Isabel chased by the lustful shepherd Aristaeus, who bore the Crichton coat of arms—lion rampant azure on field argent—emblazoned on his tunic; it was Isabel stung by the serpent and swept off by her phantom lover. Like Orpheus, Robert sought for his missing queen, only to find her in the Hades of a leper house. No matter how long or how sweetly he sang, the lord of this underworld would not release his Eurydice.

Robert woke with a start to the abbey bells summoning the brothers to matins. It was only four o'clock, yet the spring sunlight was already beginning to seep into the window of his cell. After hasty devotions, Robert mounted the stool at his writing desk, put aside the poem he had been toying with, and took a piece of parchment he had recently scraped clean for re-use. He reflected long enough only to warm his fingers by blowing on them, then began to write: "Here begins the treatise of Orpheus, King, and how he went to heaven and to hell to seek his Queen."

He recounted the divine lineage of Orpheus—the marriage between his mother Calliope, the muse of epic poetry, the "finder of all harmony," and Apollo, the god of the arts. He explained how, because of the musician's noble stature and manhood, Eurydice, the Queen of Thrace, became enamored of him. He described their wedded joy. And the fading of that joy, "Like to a flower that pleasantly will spring, which fades so soon and ends with such mourning."

He described how Orpheus poured his complaint out to his harp when his queen was taken by Proserpine, the "goddess infernal," to hell:

"O doleful harp, with many mournful string,
Turn all thy mirth and music into grieving
And cease of all thy subtle songs so sweet.
Now weep with me, thy lord and woeful king,
Which lost has in earth all his liking."

How Orpheus sang his prayers to the same gods who had condemned Cresseid, but in reverence, not rebuke. And how he learned the harmony of the spheres, so that he could lull to sleep Cerberus and the Furies, guardians of Hell, and thus relieve the tortures of its inhabitants with his divine music. He caused the wheel to cease turning long enough for Ixion to escape, he held the waters long enough for Tantalus to drink, he released Titius from the grip of the bird that tore at his liver each day.

When writing of Orpheus' first glimpse of the dead Eurydice, Robert shuddered. It had been one thing to describe the leper Cresseid with the detachment of one who gave alms to an unknown. But it was Isabel he saw before him now:

Lean and deathlike, piteous and pale of hue,
Right wan and sickly, withered as the weed.
Her lily skin was like unto the lead.

For playing such exquisite music, Orpheus could, the King of Hades promised, take his queen back with him, but with this provision—that the musician not look back at her until they had reached the upper world. Just as they were about to reach sunlight, Orpheus turned his head. Only slightly, just enough to glimpse his beloved's form, to make certain that she was following him. They were close enough now to fulfilling the command. What could be the harm? But with that single glance in that single moment, all happiness vanished.

Thus followed the narrator's love lament, with its catalogue of oxymorons:

What art thou, Love? How shall I thee define?
Bitter and sweet? cruel and merciful?
Pleasing to some, while others complain and pine?
To some constant, to others variable?
Hard is thy law, thy bonds unbreakable;
Who serves thy law, though he be never so true,

Perchance, sometime, he shall have cause to rue.

Robert scratched away the hours of the morning until class began, and then the hours of the twilight. For a fortnight he penned his way after Orpheus, through earth and heaven and hell. He paused only for his classes, for the midday meal, for Sunday mass, for brief hours of sleep. His mind toiled while the boys came before him, one by one, to recite in halting phrases their translations. Often as not, he was off somewhere in the land of Thrace or even in Hades, straining to find words of his own, so that when they had finished, the boys waited like doomed souls in the Apocalypse of St. John, after the breaking of the seventh seal, wondering what the long silence portended.

Robert avoided conversation with everyone, but especially with Father Charles. He could feel Charles' stare follow him in the refectory, and once they inadvertently caught each other's eyes at Mass. But Robert quickly lowered his gaze and escaped to his cell afterwards.

At the end of the two weeks, he had completed the story itself. There was yet a *moralitas* to append, but that could wait. A scholarly audience would demand such an allegorical interpretation of the myth. For the sake of the one who had inspired his poem, however, he was finished.

Robert made two copies the poem in his notary's fairest hand. One he folded into a packet and with the following letter tied it for delivery by Brother Benedict.

> To Dame Isabel Inglis, greetings.
>
> I cannot hope to receive your forgiveness for my brutish actions. Yet I beseech you to accept this trifle as a poor token of my grief and mortification.
>
> Permit me, I beg you, to visit you again.
>
> Your humble and contrite servant,
> Robert Henryson

A fortnight later he received a reply. It was this letter that he kept bound with his Orpheus, together with Isabel's first and with the queen's.

> You can appreciate, I trust, the difficulty writing now affords me, but this I set forth in my own hand that I openly and freely forgive

you and just as openly and freely welcome a visit from one I have ever admired.

Your Isabel

That night Robert slept as one dead.

The following Sunday, after Mass, found Robert once more making his way to Stirling. A steady drizzle that morning had turned the Dunfermline streets to mud, and though the rain had ceased, the chill it had brought with it remained. Long before Robert reached the leper house, he was soaked through, and the hem of his gown was splotched with mud kicked up by his mule.

The sisters, who had been apprised of his coming, produced a dry gown, a clean pair of hose, slippers, and a fleece-lined cloak, along with a mug of warmed honey and whiskey. As he sat down beside the fire, the drink took effect almost immediately, fortifying him for the encounter soon to come. From the small window to the adjoining room, the raspy voice he expected and half feared spoke.

"It's not so fine a day as when you first came, but I'm just as glad to see you."

Robert started from his seat. "O Isabel."

"Do not be worrying. I've worn a veil this time. It's firmly fixed; the sisters have seen to that." A hoarse laughter, muffled by the cloth, seemed to emanate from elsewhere in the chamber, as if disembodied.

"I am so ashamed."

"You need not be. I've long since lost my own shame." When Robert was silent, she added, "Are you afraid I am not sorry enough for my sins of twenty years ago? There's many a sin that's joined them since, and I have not time enough to be recounting them all. The sisters see to that."

Robert's mind was drawn away from the veil and bandages. Isabel's tone frightened him. Frightened him first for her soul. He, too, had long since put his youthful sins out of mind. But were some sins so appalling that they should never be put out of mind? Was not her illness a continuous reminder, the means to a perpetual penance? How could she call into question teaching of St. Paul about the purity of the body? And what about the best thinking of the Church Fathers, from St. Jerome onwards? Isabel had slipped off the first rung on the ladder of perfection.

But Robert was frightened for another reason. Somehow, he feared, all of this was linked to that which had attracted him to the young Isabel—

her energy and independence, yes, even a certain defiance that was more seductive to him than any of the charms he saw worked upon the young (and not so young) on market days.

Isabel seemed to read his fears but did little to ease them. "I weep each time I read your Cresseid, and I read it often. But while it makes for fine reading, it does not do so well for living."

Her words stung. Isabel noticed his astonishment and laughed again. "It's little you'll be knowing about women if you expect their lives to end when Fortune is not so kind to them."

"And was it only Fortune, then?" Robert blurted the question out.

"You said so yourself." The laughter, which had not ceased, was now tinged with mockery. "Your Cresseid's a wonder and no mistake. But as your Cato taught me, even though I read much, I must not believe much of what I read because you poets sing of the marvelous."

Robert nodded, despite himself. "Aye, *multa legas facito, perlectis neglege multa; nam miranda canunt, sed non credenda poetae.*"

"Well, then, am I supposed to make an exception in the case of my master's miraculous stories? Still, I am grateful that you sought me in this hell. I could be pleased to hear some more of your music." Robert listened for the laughter, but none came. Isabel had read his Orpheus.

In that moment, Robert was overcome by the simplicity of her gratitude, by a renewed feeling of shame, by his own gratitude for her forgiveness. He wept. Isabel laid a bandaged hand on the sleeve of his gown, careful not to touch his arm. So overcome was he that he unthinkingly took it in both of his own hands and held it to his cheek.

"No. You must not." Robert felt a tremor as Isabel sought to withdraw her hand from his. He then became aware of what he had done. Father Charles' boisterous laughter echoed in his mind and he smiled. He grasped her hand even more firmly and pressed it to his lips. It was her turn to weep.

It could not have been more than a moment that they remained this way, standing silently at the small opening, their eyes closed, her hand motionless in his. That moment seemed to draw into itself all the years of their separation and Robert sought to read in the spongy contours of her bindings all that Isabel had felt and become in the meanwhile. She tugged once more and this time he gently released her.

"So, the famous Master Robert Henryson, consort of kings and queens, Chaucer newly raised from the grave." Isabel stood back to examine him. Robert bowed grandly with an exaggerated sweep of his arm. "You little knew that I read your first poems, did you? Aside, of course, from 'The Reasoning Between Age and Youth,' by which you bestowed on us bairns, my brothers and me, the wisdom of your advanced age. Were you yet twenty-five then?" She coughed slightly, then called up from memory the description of Age:

> A caitive on a staff,
> With cheeks so lean and locks ragged and hoar,
> With hollow eyes, and hoarse his voice; and wan,
> Withered, and weak he was as any wand.
> A sign he bore upon his breast above
> In letters true and firm, with this legend:
> "O youth thy flowers fade as soon as love."

Robert blushed. "You're mocking me." He could feel Isabel smile beneath her veil. Without answering him, she began to recite again:

> But look on this letter and learn if ye can
> The practice and points of this apothecary.
> If you minister this medicine at night to some man,
> E're morning be past, my powder, I swear,
> He shall bless you or else bitterly you ban,
> For it shall flee from his womb, either up or down there.
> Beware when ye gather those weeds and grass,
> Either sweet or sour,
> That it be in a good hour.
> It is a dark mirror,
> Another man's bare ass.

Robert's blush deepened even further. "O aye, I read others. 'Some Practices of Medicine' was, I think, my poor father's favorite. He had little use for doctors, though he called on them all the time. How shocked he would have been if he had known his maiden daughter had read of men's bums."

Alexander Inglis' hypochondria was legendary among his fellows. Physicians both repelled and attracted him. If he had a money pouch for every urinal he had filled for them, he would possess a king's ransom. Yet he read widely on the subject—especially the Greek Galen and the Arab Avicenna—and offered diagnoses of his own condition to those only too willing to receive his gold for his own advice. Alexander was delighted with Robert's lampoon, with its apothecary's shop full of imaginary drugs. Isabel seemed to relish the thought of shocking not only her father, but also her former tutor.

Isabel's father had stipulated that the tutor of his children should have facility in poetry. Robert had duly impressed him with his religious allegory "The Bloody Shirt," which he had submitted for inspection at the interview. But on nights when Alexander hoisted a dram or two beyond his limit, he pressed Robert for more earthy fare. It occurred to Robert then, that there were other poems he would not have had the children see. Certainly the father had been more circumspect than to leave *all* the poems about. But no, Isabel began to recite more of his verses:

> "Makyne, the night is soft and dry;
> The weather is warm and fair;
> And the green wood right near us by
> To walk around everywhere.
> There may no gossip us espy,
> Who to love is no friend.
> Therein, Makyne, both ye and I
> Unseen our sweet love spend."

> "Robin, that world is all away
> And quite brought to a close;
> And never again thereto, by faith,
> Shall it be as thou chose.
> For of my pain thou made it play
> And all in vain I pled.
> As thou hast done, so shall I say,
> 'Mourn on.'" Away she sped.

"Would I be over bold in assuming that the Robin in the tale is your own self?" Isabel asked when she finished.

"Over bold indeed."

Isabel ignored his response and continued, "Who might the Makyn have been, I'm wondering."

"You may wonder all you wish. There's a reason that we Scots call poets 'makars.' A makar does that very thing—he makes. You'll not be finding a person of flesh and blood behind every name you read."

"But if you imagine such a one, is she not as good as flesh and blood? Do her thoughts not give her life? It was not so easy to listen to my Master Robert lecture us on the distichs of Cato when I kept wondering how strong Makyn's song had been—or still was."

"That poem was the toy of a foolish young man."

"Aye, and a foolish lass read it." Isabel sighed.

She did not have to elaborate for Robert to suspect that there had been some of Makyn in Isabel. Had he, out of pride in his ability to amuse her father with such "toys," as he called them, inadvertently laid a weapon in her hands? How many Robins had his Makyn wounded with it? One only had to look at her to see how deeply she had wounded herself. "I'd be pleased if you would forget it," he pleaded.

"I am not likely to hurt myself on it now. Besides, it delights me, and I would keep it close by." She pointed toward her head. "It's locked away here." When he frowned, she added, "You've nothing to fear, though. 'The Bloody Shirt' was always my favorite. The sisters sing it to us to the music of one of your pupils."

"Aye. Ingram Bannatyne."

"You must be proud."

Robert did not respond. There was much that he wished to find out about her, and she had kept the light of the conversation on him.

"Do you mind if I sit?" Isabel asked. "I do not have the strength I once had."

"By all means. Please forgive me for being thoughtless. I nearly forgot. I brought you a mince pie and a bottle of Bordeaux, which Father Charles sent along."

"Father Charles?"

"The cellarer, and my confessor."

Robert cut Isabel a slice of the pie and poured the wine into one of the tin goblets Charles had packed. He then realized that he had put her in an awkward position. The pie she could slip discreetly under her veil. But to drink, she would have much more difficulty.

"Here, let me help you." Robert reached out clumsily to lift the veil.

Isabel began to turn away. "No, please. I do not want to drive you away again."

"You'll not be driving me away—now or ever." Whatever grace had been lacking in him before armed him now. He unloosened the veil entirely and let it fall away. He gingerly raised the goblet to her damaged lips.

Isabel shivered involuntarily. "It's been a long time since I've had wine.

I'd forgotten what it tasted like."

When he had nursed a few more sips down her, Robert spoke. "We've spent over much time talking of me. How do you pass your days?" He realized how clumsy the question was, like his offer of food. Ordinary conversation was not possible with one who begged from dawn to dusk, with precious little to do otherwise because there was precious little she could do.

Isabel, it seemed, had far more important things than to hold him accountable for each misstep he made and rescued him. "Sister Martha gives us each tasks. My poor hands cannot do much fine work these days. But there are others who can spin and I can hold the yarn just so." She laughed and held out her arms in front of her. "And I sweep. I am not certain we are that helpful, but it makes us feel useful."

"The sisters are good to you, then?"

"O aye. The endowment's not great enough to feed and clothe us entirely, so we do have to beg, that's true. But even that has its rewards."

Isabel's voice grew conspiratorial and Robert had to smile. "How might that be?"

"We see grand people on the King's Highway."

"Such as?"

"Great schoolmasters, for a start, and famous poets, as well—those that read before kings and queens." When Robert blushed, Isabel added, "But we see them so often—like vermin, they are—we hardly notice them any longer." The laughter was hoarse, but distinct enough to carry Robert back to happier days when he deliberately tried to provoke her.

"O aye? And who do you watch for when you grow tired of schoolmasters and poets?"

"Great churchmen."

"Would they not be as plenteous as vermin, also?" Robert laughed.

"Aye. There are some, though—" Isabel grew serious.

"Aye?"

"Some we are pleased to see."

"Such as?"

"His Grace, William Scheves, the Archbishop of St. Andrews, passes by frequently."

"That's as it should be. No doubt the king's business calls him here often."

"Nay. That's not what I mean. Aye, he comes to Stirling on the king's business, but often as not he'll be here in disguise."

"In disguise?" Robert was incredulous.

"Aye. As a grey brother. Father Giles, master of this house, is his spiritual director. Or so we are able to surmise. The sisters tell us little. In any case, he comes here often, and when he does he ministers to us as an ordinary brother. They say he is a doctor."

That was true enough. Robert knew that Scheves had studied medicine in Louvain after leaving St. Andrews. How helpless he must have felt to come upon such wastelands as this leper hospital and to have no power to heal. Perhaps that is why he had given up the practice of medicine and had become a priest. Leave it all in the hands of God. But could anyone, even a man of Scheves' talents, be any more successful healing the body politic of the church and the state? Maybe that is why he came back to his original calling from time to time. Still, Robert was not sure that he trusted the man, though he had difficulty reading his motives or the ends he hoped to accomplish by coming to such a place.

"You know what the people say about him." Robert would have Isabel know the truth.

"I do not know what the people say. He's one of the few that will talk to us."

"They'd rather be trusting Lowrence the fox than your archbishop. '*Cucullus non monachum facit*.'"

"And if the cowl does not make the monk, does a mitre make a fox?"

Robert laughed and conceded her point. These were not the ravings of a mad person. Her story was too consistent. Still, that a man of Archbishop Scheves' stature should come so clothed. Robert was interested in this strange prelate, who could plot with earls and kings, but who would consort with lepers. The two visions seem ill-aligned. "What does he say to you?"

"He would, of course, not be speaking his heart to the likes of us. But he asks after our needs and he gives us his blessing, as if we were members of his own family. Once he even said that I reminded him of a lassie he once knew, when he was at the university." Isabel brushed some errant strands of hair from off her cheeks, tucking them into her kerchief and patting it carefully. It was as if she remembered fairer days. Robert winced at the small vanity, which only uncovered more of the welts, more of the scabs, which only highlighted the bleared and bloodshot eyes.

"He laid his hand on my head and blessed me. He no more blenched than if I had been his mother, or . . . or his wife." She sighed, and in that sigh Robert heard the burden of an age. "It was he that wrote my first letter to you, since I cannot manage so well with a quill."

One of the sisters entered the chamber that Isabel occupied and took her by the arm. "You'll be coming, my dear? The others are about to eat."

"Aye, Sister. I'm coming."

Robert handed the sister the rest of the mince pie and the bottle. "Compliments of the abbey." Taking Isabel's hand one last time, he asked, "Might I return?"

Isabel forced a laugh. "You must not stay away too long. I've not that long left."

Robert reached out and touched her cheek. She turned away, but not before he saw her eyes fill with tears. "Farewell," he whispered, and was off, lest he prolong her embarrassment.

Charles tracked him to his cell after matins the next morning. "You've been avoiding me, Robert." The beard parted into a grin like some furry Red Sea. Robert's defenses fell, as they always did, and he succumbed to the temptation to test his own undeveloped humor, a fact that never ceased to delight Charles.

"Aye, you laid a great penance on me last time we met. I can ill afford to confess to you but once a month, even less, I'm thinking. It's taken this long to unpack the burden."

Charles' appreciative laughter echoed down the stone halls. The elder monks shook their heads as they disappeared into their cells. In the paradoxical fashion of youth, the novices, who as a group were returning from a brief meditation with their novice master, either nudged one another and laughed or drew their faces into expressions of contempt for this profane man who had disrupted the holiness of their thoughts. But then what could you expect from a cellarer?

Charles was oblivious to all but Robert. "Well, the fury was upon you, and no mistake."

"The Muse." Robert corrected him. "The Muse'll be inspiring my poetry."

"Fury, muse. I cannot see the difference." Charles winked. "I'm just an ignorant brewer. But the proof's in the tasting. How was the lass liking your wine?"

Robert blushed. He had little skill in praising his own work. Only with the quill in his hand as he was composing or with his voice as he actually reciting did he feel any confidence in the merit of his work. Once such activities ceased, the poems seemed alien to him, as if written by someone else; and he had no power or desire to judge them.

"It's the lady of the feast who should be commending the wine, not the brewer."

Charles laughed again. "Then what did the lady say?"

Robert's humor left him and he grew solemn. "She prayed that Orpheus sing to her often since it is certain that she will never be released from her Hades, even under condition."

Charles, who did nothing in a small way, took Robert by the shoulders and hugged him roughly. "Then sing your heart out. There may be release for her yet."

Charles' arms relaxed. "Good night, my friend," he whispered. Tears soaked his beard, though the laughter still remained in his eyes. "Jesu give you the sleep of the righteous." With that he ambled off to his own cell, like some contented bear. Robert slept soundly that night, if not as one of the righteous, then as one of the forgiven. His dreams were of Isabel the girl singing snatches from his "Bloody Shirt" set to Ingram's music.

> The lady mourned and made great moan;
> Scarce might she hold her heart:
> "No other love loved I but one
> That dolefully now is hurt.
> God! had only my life from me been taken,
> Ere I had seen yon sight,
> Or else in begging ever to go
> Forth with yon courteous knight."
>
> He said, "Fair lady, now must I die
> Truly ye me trow.
> Take ye my shirt that is bloody
> And hang it before you.
> First think on it and then on me
> When men come you to woo."
> The lady said, "By Mary free
> Thereto I make a vow."

The dream was so vivid that Robert awoke. If Jesu had shown mercy to one woman taken in adultery, mightn't he be merciful to one more? If he had cured ten lepers at one time, migtn't he could heal one more? Mightn't he, Jesu's servant, move a mountain and deliver her from that wretched place, whole and fair as when she was young?

"Grant me the faith," Robert prayed.

X

The Toad and the Mouse

"What's wrong with Augustina? I just saw her shaking a wet paw—" Charles had brought the evening round of ale and broth. He looked down at the puddle on the floor. "Ah, I take it you did not want her company. I hope I get no such cheerless greeting."

"I've wee friends nesting under my bed. Disturb them and it'll be a wet beard you'll be shaking." Robert smiled weakly from his bed where he had settled. "So mind the door."

While balancing the bowl and mug, Charles pressed against the door with his backside, twisting his foot to an awkward angle to hold the cat at bay.

"Augustina'll be reporting you to Abbot George for harboring unlawful guests. You'd keep her from her duty." Charles brought the dinner to Robert's side. "I know you do not want this, but Cook insists."

"I'm grateful to you both. It's just—"

"Aye, I understand. Just sip on your ale while I empty this." Charles picked up the chamber pot and made for the door. In doing so, he knocked the lid awry. "Whew!" he exclaimed.

"You'll not have much longer to tend to either end of my body."

"Aye, and Jesu be praised!" Charles muttered and opened the door.

"Mind Augustina."

"Aye, my lord. Your obedient servant, my lord." Charles snorted but blocked the open doorway with his sandaled foot. He returned a few moments later with the empty pot and looked about for something to do. "I see you've been tidying up. Do you not want my company?"

"Have you no chores of your own to tend?"

"It's too late in the day for that. Besides, Abbot George has given me an assistant. To help me in my old age, you know. A young lay brother, hardly more than a boy. Fergus, his name is. I swear he does not know the difference between wine and vinegar. You're wise to be passing on when you are."

Charles picked up the manuscript of the fables and drew up a chair. He untied the ribbon. "I believe I shall read some more to you."

"Careful now. I'll not want to have spent the afternoon in vain."

"Away with your bother."

Robert lay back and closed his eyes. Just the sound of Charles' voice comforted him. The man he had taught to read now read to him:

> Upon a time, as Aesop did report,
> A little mouse came to a river side:
> She might not wade, her shanks were so short;
> She could not swim; she had no horse to ride.
>
> "Help over! Help over!" this poor mouse did cry,
> "For God's dear love, somebody, over the brim."
> With that an ugly toad, in the water by,
> Put up her head and on the bank did climb,
> Which by nature could dunk and gaily swim.
> With voice full rough, she said on this manner:
> "Good morn, Dame Mouse! What is your errand here?"
>
> "Do you see," asked she, "of yon corn so fat,
> Of plump oats ripe, of barley, peas, and wheat?
> I am hungry, and fain would be thereat,
> But I am hindered by this water great;
> And on this side I get no thing to eat
> But hard nuts, which with my teeth I bore:
> Were I beyond, my feast were far the more.
>
> "I have no boat; here is no mariner;
> And though there were, I have no freight to pay."

Charles read of the toad's offer to ferry on her back the mouse across and of the mouse's loathing of the toad's "withered face, wrinkled cheeks, loose lips, hanging brows, bow legs, and leathery hide." Such characteristics, according to the science of physiognomy, betokened "falseness and envy" because, as "the old proverb" says: "*lorum distortum vultum sequitur distortio morum*—an evil character is the source of an evil countenance."

The toad countered with her own proverb, "Thou should not judge a man after his face," and went on to explain:

> "Though I unwholesome be to look upon,
> I know not why I should rejected be?
> Were I as fair as jolly Absolon,
> I am not the source of that beauty;
> This difference in form and quality
> Almighty God has caused, through dame Nature,
> To imprint and set in every creature."

The toad might have continued indefinitely thus, but she was interrupted. "Let be thy preaching," said the hungry mouse. After the toad pledged that she would cause the mouse no harm, they bound themselves to one another and they launched out to the middle of the stream.

But the mouse's forebodings proved to be justified. The toad forswore herself and began to drown her passenger, who began to fight "till at the last she cried out for a priest." A passing hawk saw the struggle, grabbed them both, and disemboweled them.

Robert drifted in and out of consciousness as Charles read. The death of the poor mouse had sent his mind back to the spring of 1482, but not to Isabel's death. Not yet. His return to her was to be delayed by some two or three months, and until then she lingered on. No, others were to be called to the eternal kingdom first...those younger and more whole than she.

Several days after his trip to the spital house in Stirling, late in the afternoon, a knock came on Robert's cell door.

"Enter." He spoke more sharply than he intended. His Muse, or Fury, as Charles called her, had become even more importunate. The Orpheus, rather than exhaust his powers, had only inspired him further. He was crafting a few lines of verse between the end of lessons and the beginning of the evening meal. Such times were precious to him, and most in the abbey knew better than to interrupt.

"Master Robert?"

Robert knew the voice immediately and turned to face Ingram Bannatyne. It had been only four months since Robert had last seen the young man, but he had undergone yet another dramatic transformation. Although his gown was even more sumptuous, he had lost much weight and his face was haggard. His eyes betrayed his despair. Robert rose to shake hands, but Ingram brushed past his outstretched arm and embraced his former master instead.

"What is it?" Robert asked. "What's wrong?"

"I'm afraid, Master Robert, and I did not know whom to turn to. You know how Brother Martin gets. George suggested that I come talk to you."

Robert indeed knew how fussy Martin could become, even to the point of helplessness. The boys would confide in their choirmaster because he comforted them like a mother hen. Robert they found to be more practical.

"Sit down." Robert guided Ingram to a chair. "Tell me about it. Just last December you were the pride of court. What cause might there be for the king's intimates to fear anything?"

"That's just it."

"What's 'just it'?"

"The king has been pleased to consider me worthy of his attention, and as a consequence I've drawn less welcome attention."

"From whom? Make yourself plain, man."

"The Earl of Mar, for one."

Robert was still perplexed.

"Thomas Cochrane, whom you saw at the banquet on Childermas."

"The chancellor?"

"Aye, the king has made him Earl of Mar."

"But is that possible? I've heard that Cochrane is a capable man, but to make a stonemason a chancellor and then an earl? That overtaxes belief."

"O, it is possible, and it is true. Now Cochrane is the virtual tyrant of the king's household." Ingram drew a deep breath. "That's not all. The nobility, especially the Earl of Angus, are furious. It were bad enough, they say, that the king cast his pearls before such swine, but that he adorn them in pearls? That's beyond bearing."

"Whom, besides Cochrane, would Angus call swine?"

"All who eat at the king's trough." Ingram shook his head. "It is reported that his lordship, the Earl of Angus, and the others wait only the opportunity to exact vengeance."

"What about George? Is he threatened as well?"

"He does not think so. His connection with the Crichtons keeps him safe, or so he trusts. I'm not so sure. His uncle, the Lord Crichton, got the king's sister with child."

"The one who was engaged to the English earl—who is it?"

"The Earl Rivers, aye. The affair has ruined the treaty with England. I fear George is not so safe as he feels. But he has no family. I do, Master Robert."

"Dame Agnes."

"Aye, and one bairn with a second on its way. I feel like the wee poor mouse who binds herself to the toad to gain passage across the stream. The toad has turned on me and I shall drown, well and truly. And all my family with me."

Robert hesitated before asking the obvious question. As Father Charles would have have reminded him, gently but firmly, it was a question that needed asking. "Can you not sever your bonds from the Earl of Mar?"

Robert knew then what the rich young ruler must have felt when our Lord directed him to sell all he possessed.

"It's his lordship's favor that keeps me in favor with the king."

"But his lordship is aptly named. He could mar you all. There are others to grant you patronage, less great, aye, but also far less dangerous. I daresay Abbot Crichton here—I could speak to him—would eagerly welcome you as assistant *magister puerorum*. Brother Martin is certain to give over his duties soon and still harbors the belief that you would be willing to succeed him."

Ingram was silent.

"There are worse things," Robert urged. "And there are other patrons."

Ingram shook his head, and in that movement Robert knew that there were other pressures—the pressures of a family that had grown accustomed to the good things that only royal patronage could purchase.

"Agnes'll be wanting her husband, not some fancy gown, if the choice must be made."

"I'll talk with her, sir."

Ingram left the abbey. He never had time to debate the issue with Agnes. Within the month Ingram's forebodings were realized. Some of the king's favorite retainers, including Cochrane, were hanging from the bridge in the Border town of Lauder. Ingram was lying dead in his own blood on the same bridge.

The news of the carnage reached Dunfermline in bits and pieces. This much was certain: while marching through the Borders to defend the southern part of his kingdom against the English, James was met by a strong party of the nobility, led by Archibald, the Earl of Angus. Angus summoned Cochrane to treat with him at Lauder church, then seized him and hanged him. The other details were much less clear.

In one version of the story, Cochrane was taken along with William Roger, the court musician, and James Hommyle, the king's tailor. The hastily arranged court, over which the king "presided," passed summary judgment on the three men. They were lined up on Lauder Bridge, nooses were placed around their necks, and one by one they were pushed off, there to dangle just feet above the River Leader, "as if walking on its waters." One messenger felt compelled to color the story.

Other accounts added to the numbers seized and hanged. Some messengers reported that not all the retainers had died: Angus had, they said, spared the life of a certain Thomas Preston because of the king's heart-rending pleas; and Hommyle the tailor was later seen to be alive.

Even the reasons for the nobles' uprising were hotly debated. Ingram had certainly not underestimated the hatred that the nobility felt towards Thomas Cochrane and the king's "familiars," as they were called. Many folk believed, however, that Cochrane and the others were scapegoats for mounting frustration with the king's policies: his circulating the plack, or "black penny," which had debased the currency; his failure to render justice personally; his obstinate refusal to hold the noble families in proper esteem. One could take his choice.

Whatever the precise details, the king now resided in Edinburgh Castle, sequestered there for his own "protection."

Robert listened intently to the reports, quizzing each messenger carefully. None had been eyewitnesses.

"Were there others—" Robert could not bring himself to complete the question.

"None hanged," came news from the relative to the servant of the Lord Gray.

Robert sighed in relief.

"Or so I heard. But there was much confusion. Some were injured in a melee."

Two travelers seeking shelter in the abbey on the same evening offered conflicting accounts.

"Several were killed in a skirmish," according to the first.

"No, just the one," argued the other.

"Have you any names?"

"No," both agreed.

Robert did not get the full story until George returned some two weeks after the incident. By that time, Abbot Crichton was also dead. "Of a broken heart," Prior Gerald was later to say. Gerald had been with the abbot at the bridge, then had followed him to Edinburgh with the king.

"George!" Robert exclaimed when he saw his former pupil. All confidence and charm had disappeared from the young man who stood before him. Gone, too, were the elegant gown and bonnet from the previous Christmas. Instead, he wore the clothing of a yeoman, coarse worsted hose and a leather jerkin.

"Master Robert." Like Ingram just weeks before, George embraced his old schoolmaster.

"Tell me what happened," Robert urged. "I've heard so many different stories."

"He's dead," George said.

"Who?" Robert asked, but George's look told him the answer.

"Ingram."

Robert motioned to a chair. "Here, sit down. Tell me about it. How did he die?"

"It was so unnecessary." George had begun to replay the scene in his mind, and words were giving way to the images. "So unnecessary."

"Tell me," Robert coaxed.

"Angus never sought his death. The same with the others: Roger and Torpichen, Andreas and Leonard. They mattered little to the earl. It was Cochrane he was after. By implicating the others, he could argue that King James was the victim of a conspiracy. In a strange way, it gave the king a means of saving face."

"But Ingram. You said that Angus did not want Ingram."

"Ingram tried to save the court musician." George shuddered at the memory. "When they hauled Roger to the bridge, Ingram turned to me and to John, who was sitting next to Angus, recording the proceedings, as if it were a legitimate court. 'George,' he cried. 'John.' John started to rise, but the earl laid a hand on his shoulder. I ran to follow Ingram. But it was too late. He threw himself at the sergeant who was about to push Roger off the bridge. The sergeant heard the commotion, turned around, and lifted his sword in surprise. Ingram ran upon the naked blade. I could see it, Master Robert. Its point just appeared out his back."

George was crying, but his words flowed as freely as his tears. "I drew my own sword and ran at the man. Somebody grabbed me before I could do him harm. He had not even pulled his sword from Ingram's body, but had let go of it, as if the hilt would scorch his hand. For a time Ingram just stood there quivering. Then he crumpled down. I shook myself free and knelt over him. He looked up with his one good eye, but it was as if he were straining to see something beyond me. There was nothing I could do. Nothing. The earl stepped over Ingram's body as if it were a bundle of hay, and then put his boot into Roger's backside to push him off the bridge."

Robert arose and cradled the young man's head. By this point he was weeping as well. "They would have hanged me, too." George sobbed.

Robert stiffened, took George's shoulders, and held him at arm's length.

"Aye, that they would. It was my uncle, the Lord Crichton, who got the king's sister with child."

"So Ingram told me."

"Ah, that's right. I urged him to come see you."

"So your uncle did indeed ruin the English alliance?"

"Aye, and now he's in hiding. I fear the king was biding his time to rid himself of me. Of all whom the rebels hanged, I was the only one whose death he would have been glad of."

"Then why didn't they?"

"Because my father intervened."

"Your father?" The words were more an exclamation than a question.

"Aye. Abbot Crichton is…was my father."

"Holy Jesu" was all that Robert could utter.

"To spare my life he confessed his shame. It's that which killed him."

"But—" Robert didn't even know how to frame the question.

"He was the Lord Crichton's nephew. It was Abbot Henry that got my mother with child, sometime before he became abbot. At one stroke he risked losing any chance of reconciliation with his uncle and preferment in Holy Church, which he had so fought for by reason of his own bastardy. The Lord Crichton, who knew nothing of all this, agreed that I was to be called an orphan, brought up as one of his own family. When I came of age, my father urged his lordship to allow me to attend the abbey school. There I might be under my father's watchful eye all the while."

"And you nor his lordship none the wiser."

"Aye."

Suddenly, the abbot's behavior towards George made sense. He was one of those fathers who would punish rather than indulge, who would hold his own child to higher standards than those expected of others, perhaps even impossible standards. The ruthlessness with which Henry had dealt with his son's trespass was no attempt to break his spirit, but to instill in him a hardness that would survive the rough world of court intrigue. How it must have pained him to live all those years in silence, first without being able to pull his son to him, then with that son's rejection. How great that love must have remained to destroy all he had to save that son's life.

"And your mother?"

"He could not tell."

"You asked him?"

"Aye."

"He could not, or he would not?"

"He could not. That was part of his shame and sorrow, as well. She pledged that she would never haunt him if only he would ensure that I was taken care of. She kept her word and he did not know where she was or how she was or whether she were still alive. It was one thing to be an orphan. But a bastard and an orphan?" George paused. "Still, I would not trade places with poor Ingram."

"What about his widow and child?"

"The good Queen Margaret has arranged for them to live at Stirling Castle, at least till the child is born and they have a place to settle."

"And your own self?"

"There's no place for me at court. I've come seeking Prior Gerald's blessing to enter the novitiate."

"And is that what you want?"

"I am not certain. But I'm hoping to find some peace."

Robert nodded. He feared that George would be disappointed. People, he knew, tended to bring their peace or trouble with them. That much Charles and his own experience had taught him. But he wouldn't begrudge the young man the attempt. George had had enough to sift through without Robert's adding to his load.

Robert changed the subject. "And John?"

"All happened so quickly afterward. Off the others went from the bridge, and then it was my turn. All the while, whenever I looked in John's direction he never raised his head, but just kept writing, writing. That's when my father, that is, Abbot Henry, intervened. Since then, I've seen John only twice, but each time he has turned away." George shook his head. There was no more to be said. He rose to leave. "Thank you, Master Robert. A strange thing it is to say, but I feel as if I've come home." He embraced Robert and then left.

Charles looked over at his friend. It appeared that Robert had gone to sleep. Since he was nearly finished with the fable, Charles read on through the end.

> The hawk is death, that comes forth suddenly
> As does a thief, and cuts off soon the battle.
> Be vigilant therefore, always ready,
> For man's poor life is brittle and mortal.
>
> Adieu, my friend, and if anyone inquires
> Of this fable, so shortly I conclude,
> Say thou, I left the rest unto the friars,
> To make example or similitude.
> Now Christ for us that died upon the rood,
> Of soul and life as thou art our Savior,
> Grant us to pass into a blessed hour.

Charles smiled at his friend's dry humor that betrayed an otherwise stern view of the world. At some 400 lines, the last fable of the Toad and the Mouse was hardly short. But the penchant of friars to spin out elaborate allegories from the simplest of stories was a standing joke among the Benedictine brothers. If St. Benedict had admonished his disciples to pray and to work—"*Orare et laborare*"—it would appear that somewhere St. Dominic had given his friars scope to belabor a point—"*Laborare et belaborare.*"

Charles neatly lay the manuscript down on the desk and blew out the lamp.

XI

The Lack of Wise Men

The click of the latch as Charles left brought Robert back to the present. So busily had his mind been racing, he had hardly been aware that he was asleep, if sleeping it were. Again, his memory had been fighting against the stillness of death. Was this simply its way of cramming in every last bit of life before extinction? Or was this to be the way of things as he moved into Christ's kingdom? Would he even be aware that he was "gone," that what he now termed memory would be his eternal present? These imponderables ceased to be ponderous. He could no longer get out of bed to write. His work there was over. His legs would carry him as far as the chamber pot and back, just a matter of feet, inches really, and no further.

The events at Lauder Bridge that summer had stirred up in him all that frustrated and grieved him in the practice of the law. He had subsequently written out his anger at John and John's masters in a poem that lamented the state of poor Scotland.

> That former age when ruled the king Saturn,
> For goodly governance this world was golden called;
> For untruth we knew not whereto it turns;
> The time that Octavian, the monarch, could hold,
> O'er all was peace, well set as men's hearts would:

Then reigned just rule, and reason held his sway;
Now wanes prudence, nobility is thralled;
For lack of wise men, fools now have their way.

Where might justice dwell with equity?
Good is not praised, nor punished is trespass;
All men lead lawless lives at liberty,
Not ruled by reason, more than ox or ass;
Good faith has flown, virtue is frail as glass,
True love is lost, falseness gainst truth inveighs.
Such wickedness for governance may pass.
For lack of wise men, fools now have their way.

Robert had been forced to delay his return to Isabel. To begin with, there were the ordinary matters of the abbey to attend to. Drawing up bequests and deeds in trust, preparing for the renewal of tacks in Whitsuntide, settling boundary disputes or the rights to pasturage, taking depositions for the archdeacon's consistory court. Then there was the turmoil in the kingdom and, consequently, at the abbey.

By the time he did visit the leper house again, Isabel was too weak to meet Robert as before, in the receiving chamber. He was, instead, led to her chamber. He was shocked at the change.

"You've come back," she whispered from her bed.

"O Isabel. I little thought—"

"Do not be bothered. I'm glad to see you."

"But had I known—"

"My condition? I'm dying, Master Robert, and have been these many months. You need not step so lightly around my feelings. I knew you would come when you could; and if I missed you, certainly we would see one another again under happier circumstances."

"Happier circumstances indeed." Robert began to weep.

Isabel attempted to sit up. "Something's happened. Tell me."

Robert took her hand and sat on the stool that the sisters had provided him. He recounted George's story.

"So the news was true."

"You've heard, then?"

"Not all you've told me, certainly not about poor Ingram, but we're not so isolated here as you think. There's a good deal of gossip to be reaped on the King's Highway."

Robert shook his head. "Before I saw him for the last time, Ingram told me he felt like the mouse tied to the frog."

"So as to cross the stream?"

"Aye. Cochrane was his ferry to greatness. Ingram remembered the other part of the fable—that a hawk disemboweled them both—but he was too far out in the stream to hide."

"And George, what happened to him?" Isabel asked.

"It's almost beyond believing." Robert stared at the bandaged hand as he told the rest of the sad tale. "It would have torn your heart to hear him." He looked up to see that Isabel's heart had been torn. She was crying.

"So he's to become a monk?"

"Aye."

"Bring him to me," she whispered.

"What?"

"Bring George to me."

"Why? Why should he come?"

"Say it's a dying woman's request. It will be his first act of corporal mercy in the Lord's service."

"I don't understand, Isabel."

"Don't you now?"

"No. Tell me."

Isabel shook her head. "Your Cresseid left her testament. Perhaps I can bequeath mine to this poor young man—in place of the son that was taken from me. It is not much, but as you're a notary, it can be all legal like." She smiled. "You must not tarry, short of the apocalypse."

"I'll bring him."

"Soon?"

"Aye, soon."

"Bless you, Robert."

Prior Gerald was reluctant to grant Robert leave and more especially George, who was still a young novice. "It's highly irregular, Master Robert. The young man has just joined the abbey and already you'll be disrupting his training."

"I understand, Prior Gerald. But she's dying."

"That makes it even more irregular. A leper woman, requesting to see someone she does not even know."

"She has nothing left, and he's little better off. Perhaps if they join his poor loaf with her wee fish, the Lord might multiply it."

Gerald relented. "I'll pray for that miracle, then."

Robert was grateful that for all the administrative demands placed on Prior Gerald since Abbot Henry's death, the old man had never lost his faith that the real work of the abbey was prayer.

Before Robert could set off, Prior Gerald called him into his office. Without speaking, Gerald shoved a piece of parchment across his desk. Robert knew that Gerald was seldom moved to anger. It was his tranquility that must have absorbed the initial shocks of Abbot Henry's angers and tempered their execution. Robert looked at the opening.

> *Omnibus ad quos praesentes literae pervenerint, salutem in Domino sempiternam.*
>
> I, Alexander, Duke of Albany and loving and loyal brother to his royal majesty, King James, the third of that name, do wish to give honest account of those proceedings, recently enacted at Lauder Bridge this May last, that all backbiters and troublers of the king's peace may at once be silenced and that order and good will be quickly restored to this unhappy kingdom.

It was the official report of the events at Lauder. Every archbishop, bishop, abbot, and abbess, every earl and baron, every sheriff and bailie to whom it was circulated knew, however, that it was the work of Archibald, Earl of Angus. Those sympathetic to Angus and his disaffected nobles read the proclamation aloud in chapter houses or market squares. Those who saw the hanging of the king's advisors as sedition followed the letter of the command and merely posted the document, to weather away under the rain and the illiterate gaze of the townsfolk. The document had been addressed to Abbot Henry, who had died before it was delivered. Prior Gerald had not yet made it public.

"Read it," the prior said.

Robert sat down and began the sad task.

> Our most royal king, having hastily made choice of such to be about him as would not correct, but approve all his sayings, and who would not offend him by gainsaying, but did curry favor by soothing of him and who with flattering admiration did extol all that he said or did; and having thereby excluded the faithful nobility from his counsel, found himself wholly at the devotion of a few of his servants with whom he advised and consulted of all business and either followed their opinions or made them to consent, and

execute his will.

Robert skimmed through the list of those hanged: Cochrane, Roger, Andreas. He shook his head when he found saw that Roger was "thought to have been the king's pander, and an enticer of him to lewdness and wronging his Queen."

"Thought to have been," he snorted. No word yet of Ingram. He skipped to Douglas' speech before the convocation of lords:

> "My honorable lords, I hold it not needful to go about with many words to set before you the estate of this kingdom. You who are the arms and limbs of this kingdom are left without a head, as a ship without a pilot and master, exposed to the storms and tempests of fortune. His Majesty, a man indeed (if he were himself) of a generous mind and rare understanding, bewitched in his affection, asks no advice or counsel of his nobility, but consults with a few base, vile, and ignorant fellows, who fill his sick mind with vain fear and superstition. Our contentions have not been for our lives, but for the honor and empire of Scotland. A noble heart, as it is easily mitigated by prayer and entreaty; and even with the consideration of the instability of human affairs it is moved to pity and compassion, so it is vehement and violent against those that oppose it. What you shall resolve to do, I pray God to prosper."

Robert recognized in the address the handiwork of a skilled incendiary. The earl could not have failed to stir to violence those already convinced that violence had been done them, against their name and prerogatives. Robert continued to read.

> When the Earl had finished speaking, the Lord Gray craved audience and told the Apologue of the Mice, who, consulting in a public meeting how to be sure from the cat's surprising of them, found out a very good way, which was to hang a bell about her neck that would ring as she stepped and to give them warning of her approach. But when it came to be questioned who would undertake to tie the bell about the cat's neck, there was never a mouse that dared peep or undertake it.
>
> The Earl understood his meaning, wherefore he answered shortly, "I will bell the Cat, and what your lordships conclude to

be done, shall not lack execution."

And thus the deed was carried out, the hanging of those men, "whom the good of the King, of the Nobility, and whole Country required necessarily to be removed from their Prince." Still no word of Ingram, George, or Abbot Henry. Robert did not wish to read on but was like the serpent's victim, charmed with that which it loathed.

> Yet it was done with as great respect to the king, as it could be in such a case, where matters were to proceed contrary to his mind. The nobility granted his desire when he did intercede for his young page, John Ramsay, one of the guilty, which shows how willing they would have been to have granted the rest also, if it could have been done safely. A very remarkable and rare example of carefulness of the commonwealth, joined with all modesty, love, and dutifulness towards their King. Their behavior was just such as lawyers prescribe in such cases, who, accounting the person of the Prince sacred and not to be touched any way, do allow that their wicked counsellors and abusers only be taken order with, where the good of the country enforces it.
>
> Wherein the Earl of Angus being the principle actor, the chief commendation therefore can not be taken from him; the praise, I say, not only of wisdom in propounding and persuading, of courage and resolution in undertaking, but also of discreet moderation and dutiful regard to the King in performing of this action without tumult or uproar.
>
> Whereupon, the nobility have appointed me General Lieutenant of Scotland to aid His Majesty in all affairs pertaining to the safety and security of his person and of this realm.
>
> In testimony of which things is affixed my seal. Given this 10th day of June 1482 in the Castle of Edinburgh.

Robert hung his head. He grieved, to be sure, for his bleeding country. But his grief took on a more personal form. The Earl of Angus might have been responsible for the bitter events at Lauder Bridge; but it had been one of his own students, John de Leith, secretary to the earl, who had sugared them to make them more palatable. This was not the use for which Robert had given John words.

At last Robert composed himself sufficiently. "What will you do?" he asked Gerald.

"One thing I will not do. Post this for all the brothers to see. The effrontery of the earl and such shameless, self-serving—" Gerald could not finish his sentence. Some small, dark, unregenerate part of his being was about to break out into the light. "They forget I was there. I saw those men hanged. I saw that poor boy stabbed and treated with no more care than a piece of butchered meat. Abbot Henry was a hard man, but I saw him broken no less than if he had been hanged or stabbed. And it will be that story I tell, not some fable."

Robert feared the old man would have a stroke right then, and needlessly. Whatever protests anyone made would be blown away like so many straws in the wind. Angus and Albany would be little bothered by such gnats as Prior Gerald. Still, Robert felt a deep affection for the man. He only hoped that the abbot's successor would listen to Gerald and learn something from his sanctity. Robert concluded "Lack of Wise Men" with this prayer.

> O lord of lords, God and governor:
> All ills reform and all vice burn away;
> What is degraded, for pure pity redress.
> For lack of wise men, fools now have their way.

XII

The Garment of Good Ladies

obert had heard it said of women close to childbirth that they suddenly bestirred themselves to great industry, as if their spirits were giving birth to an idea that the child would soon animate. Such was his case now. There would be no sleep tonight, nor ever again in this life. Instead, he would keep vigil as he waited, though with a mental industry, for his own soul to be birthed into Christ's kingdom. He began to recite psalms, which, by his constant attendance at divine office over these last ten years, had dyed nearly his every thought. It was the Psalms he had read to Isabel in her last hours. He and George.

Robert never told George of Angus' account of the events at Lauder, nor of the proclamation naming the Duke of Albany governor, nor of his suspicion as to John's hand in their composition. He left it to George to find out such matters on his own. On their way to Stirling, they spoke of other things.

"She was one of your pupils, then?" It was George who first broached the issue of Isabel.

"Aye, the first, along with her brothers."

"That would be when?"

"Some twenty years ago, now."

"A long time. She must have been special to you."

"No more than others." Robert smiled. "No more than yourself."

George refused to be put off. "You've corresponded with her ever since?"

"Nay, not until just a few months ago. She heard that I had recited my 'Cresseid' before the king and queen and wrote to congratulate me."

"Did she read it?"

"Aye."

"And she liked it?"

"She said she did. You're certainly full of questions."

George was silent for a time, as if meditating on the most appropriate way to ask his next question. "Why did you leave?"

"What?" Robert had heard the question, but bought some few seconds to form his answer.

"Why did you leave tutoring if it's what you came back to do?"

"My work at the Inglis household was finished." He was about to add that Alexander Inglis had determined thus, but it would have been a lie. "Besides, it was the law I thought I'd been called to."

"What kind of pupil was she?"

"A good deal brighter than her brothers. She would have made a fine scholar, had she been a man and thus had the chance."

"Like Heloise."

The words took Robert by surprise. They fell on his ears like the echo of Father Ninian's voice reverberating over the span of years. He was about to protest his innocence, but shot a glance at George to determine if any greater meaning lay beneath the surface. The young man's gaze was fixed ahead. The phrase was innocent enough.

Robert breathed more easily. "Aye, like Heloise."

"Is she beautiful, this Isabel of yours?"

Robert had waited for the right time to tell George about what was awaiting them. All he had said was that she was ill, seriously ill. "She was little more than a wisp of a lass when I left." Robert's memory fixed on the moment her father had presented her at Crichton Castle. "She was just beginning to blossom."

"Certainly you can remember something."

Robert smiled sadly. George was creating a portrait of this unknown woman in his mind. "I suppose you could call her lovely—not beautiful, but lovely." He added, "The disease will have wasted her."

"Is she a leper then?" The words came out matter-of-factly.

Robert shuddered. "Aye. She's a leper."

"Would she be looking like your Cresseid, then?"

"Aye."

George seemed unperturbed by the news. "What I cannot figure is why she would want to see me."

"She knows about Lauder."

"You've spoken to her about me?"

"Aye. And of poor Ingram and John. She knows the whole story. For some reason, she thinks she might bring you some comfort. She's dying, George. I could not bring myself to gainsay her."

"I understand."

Robert let the response go. How could George understand much of anything? Isabel's request? Even he, Robert, did not really understand that. Or Robert's inability to refuse that request? But the young man seemed not to be bothered. He seemed content to accept that mystery was at the heart of most things human. That in itself was a profound understanding. The events at Lauder had changed him.

They reached the spital house shortly after their midday meal. Most of the other lepers—those able-bodied enough to do so—were still abroad, collecting alms. A sister led the two men back to Isabel's chamber.

"I'm glad you've come when you did. She is not long for this world."

Isabel lay still on her cot. A Franciscan brother was kneeling by her, trying to feed her a thin soup. He rose when the others entered the room.

"May I?" Robert held out his hand for the bowl. The friar nodded slightly and gave it to him. He then left the room. Robert took the vacant place by the cot.

"I knew I'd see you again," Isabel said by way of greeting. Besides being hoarse, her voice was now weak. Robert made to feed her.

"Ach, take that from me." She feebly pushed the bowl away from her. "There will be more important things to do than eat. George? Did you bring him with you?"

"Aye. He's here."

"He'll not be frightened of me?"

"Nay." Robert stood back to let George by him. George knelt at the side of the cot and took Isabel's hand.

"It's I, Dame Isabel. George Crichton."

If he were revolted by Isabel's appearance or the dismal place in which she lay, he made no show.

Robert's shame at his own first meeting with Isabel rose in him afresh.

"Let me look at you." Isabel studied George carefully. "I can see why no one suspected."

"Suspected what, madam?"

"Suspected that you were Abbot Henry's son. The resemblance is over subtle."

"You knew Abbot Henry—my father—then?"

"Long ago. Long before I became like this. Long before he became Abbot of Dunfermline."

Whatever effect these words had on George, they came as a shock to Robert. All he had ever known of Isabel were her youth and this condition, as if the change from one to the other had happened instantaneously. Then he remembered Sarah Inglis' story. Of course Isabel could have met Henry Crichton, the bastard younger brother to the Lord and thus half-uncle to Isabel's betrothed, the unfortunate Edward.

"Tell me about your father," Isabel continued.

"I never knew him as my father," George said simply. "He was always distant and aloof. Not just to me, but to all the boys."

Robert was certain that Isabel would be able to see through George's politeness. "Stern, sometimes even cruel," would have been more accurate. Still, what George had said was not a lie, and there was no need to upset Isabel with a starker rendering of the truth.

"Yet he must have loved you to have given up everything to save your life."

George shrugged, no doubt remembering that the abbot had singled him out to bully him. "Aye. It's just that we had not long to get to know one another as father and son. Sometimes—" he started, but thought better of it.

"Sometimes what?" Isabel pressed him.

"Sometimes I wish he had kept his honor and let me die with my friend."

Isabel roused herself. "O, say not so. You have been spared for some reason. Do not trample on the sacrifice of ones who gave your life to you." She relaxed. "He was hard on you. I hear it in your voice. But judge him not too harshly. There was a time when he could laugh, when he could be gentle. After my Edward died—"

Robert winced. He had no claims on Isabel, no reason after all these years to hold out any hope at all that her infatuation with him was anything but a passing fancy. Despite Father Charles' admonition and his own prayer, he had not quite let go of her intimacies with others than himself.

Isabel drew a long breath, then continued. "After my Edward died, your father came to Crichton Castle to join the other family in mourning. Although Edward's uncle, he was barely older than his nephew. Lord Crichton took no pleasure to see Henry. I never learned the reason why. There's little understanding families."

Robert thought of Samuel's anger, which had smoldered for two decades. Isabel spoke of what she knew.

"In his hurt, your father turned his attentions to me and showed me every kindness in my grief."

Isabel paused, as if too weary to continue. She was, Robert soon discovered, trying to find words to continue. "Neither of us ever meant it to happen. Of that I am certain."

It began to dawn on Robert the import of what Isabel was saying.

"On the eve of his departure, Henry came to bid me farewell."

Isabel seemed no longer to be speaking to George. She now called his father "Henry," and her voice took on that far-away sound of one ransacking her memory for treasures kept stored away.

"Lord Crichton had withdrawn all my attendants from me. Now that his son was gone, he saw that there was little reason to keep me about. It was as if Henry and I were forgotten. Left alone as we were, we found our comfort in one another. We were both embarrassed. With one last kiss he bid me the farewell he had come to give and was gone. He left behind more than he knew."

"So he was the father of the child?" Robert nearly choked on the question.

George had by this point laid his face into the bed. He was sobbing.

Isabel gently stroked his hair with her bandaged hand and looked up at Robert. "Aye. Everyone thought that Edward was the father, but we never knew one another in that way. I was too ashamed to disabuse them of the notion. At least Edward and I were betrothed. There was shame enough in that, but I could live with it. To confess to being unfaithful to his memory, and he hardly cold in the family vault, that was more than I could bear. There was Henry to think of, as well. Already the king had put forth his name for the abbacy. The scandal would turn the king's favor to wrath, and it was only this promotion that kept Henry tied to his brother at all. Lord Crichton had the family reputation to think about.

"The news broke my poor father's heart. Malcolm made ready to bring me home, but the plague took him before he could make arrangements. That left Samuel, who turned his face against me."

"And Father?" George raised his head.

130

"He came with the Lord Crichton to Edinburgh before my delivery to see that I was provided for at the Greyfriars' convent. Actually, his lordship came to deliver terms. If I gave up all rights to the child once it was born, the Crichton family would adopt it and bring it up in a life of privilege. If I refused, they would disavow all knowledge of it and I would be forced to raise it as best I could."

"Father? What did Father do?"

"I looked at him for guidance, but he lowered his eyes. I knew then I was alone."

George struck the cot. He was weeping now in grief and fury.

"You must forgive him—" she paused before she added, "Son. I have long since done so. There was little else he could do. In this way, he would be in a position to look after your education and welfare. Things just did not turn out as he hoped. As any of us hoped."

"But Sarah Inglis. She said that the bairn did not live." Robert was confused.

"The sisters gave out the story that I lost it, which, strictly speaking, was true. To me, the child was as if stillborn. I never saw him before today." She smiled weakly. "Others were left to make of that message what they would."

Isabel closed her eyes from the exhaustion of telling her story. George was now also calm. He took her hand between his and laid his head next to hers. Robert left the chamber.

Outside, Robert leaned on the short stone wall that surrounded the hospital. He gazed at a hill that rose starkly from the plain to the east of Stirling. He breathed deeply the midsummer air. There were still so many questions, but he doubted now he would ever gain the answers.

"Good day to you, Master Robert Henryson."

Robert wiped his eyes and turned to see the friar who had been feeding Isabel when he had first entered her cell.

"You'll be free to cry around me. There's enough misery here to cry about."

"How did you know my name?"

The friar joined him at the wall. Together they stared across the plain. "Your fame as a poet spreads farther than you know. Besides, I had occasion to hear you read some months since."

"I've read only once in public, outside the abbey."

"Aye, here at Stirling Castle." The friar jerked his head in the direction of the castle that loomed behind them. "I know."

131

"Then you were there?"

"Aye." The word was clipped, as if the friar were reflecting on something else. "That promontory there—aye, the one you were looking at—a fine place for a monument or cross. One could see it for miles." He then turned to look at Robert. "Your description of Cresseid's disease—you've a good eye for detail. If you can bide the sight of ones such as she, you might have been a fine doctor."

The friar's words seemed to inspire confidence. "I have not always done so well biding her sight," Robert confessed.

"So I remember. You left the evidence somewhere about here—in that ditch, as I seem to remember."

Robert turned abruptly in surprise. "Then it was you?"

The man ignored the question. "One turned stomach is of little count. It's the coming back—that's when you show your heart's gained mastery over this frail flesh. As I say, you would have made a fine doctor, had you not gone into teaching—or law."

Robert continued to stare.

The friar laughed. "Aye. Yon Isabel. She'll be often talking about you. And about George and Abbot Henry."

"Then you know?"

"Aye. I've exhausted my poor skill and there's little else I can do to ease her body. Perhaps I have brought some comfort to her spirit."

Robert looked at the friar keenly. The face was vaguely familiar, although Robert knew he had seen it no more than once or twice.

"Perhaps you'll be remembering some words about a swallow preaching to other birds?" The friar smiled.

Robert fell to his knees before the disguised archbishop, William Scheves. "Your Grace, pardon me. I did not recognize you."

"I'd have been sorry if you had."

"Isabel told me that you visited the spital house—"

"But?"

"But I did not believe her."

"Because you thought she was mad? Dementia is not a symptom of the disease. At least the kind that Isabel has."

"She has told me little of her suffering."

"That would be her way. For all her words, it's others she'll be talking about." Scheves paused, then continued. "Besides, hers is the kind of suffering that must be borne in silence."

"What do you mean?"

"It's the judgment of others, as well, that is perhaps the heaviest to bear."

Robert thought of his own unspoken judgments. He had told himself that he feared for her soul, journeying out into eternity with unconfessed, unrepented sin. But was it his own desire to absolve her? His own satisfaction, not hers, he wished her to make? Then he remembered Samuel. How great that burden must have been upon her all these years.

"I cannot be saying what the judgment of God is in any given life. You know your Boethius. Those with the greatest power or riches or fame are often the most unhappy. If anyone should know, it would be I. I would not wish Isabel's disease on anyone, but I'll not go so far as to call it a judgment from God. He's consecrated her for himself, for some reason, and I'll not be questioning the mysteries of Providence."

"But is there not cause—?"

Scheves finished the question. "To interpret the leprosy as punishment for the sin?"

"Aye, is that not the truth of the matter?"

"As in the story of your Cresseid? No doubt some such diseases are caused by the sin you describe. Perhaps many. But I also seen times when this is not so, and—" he bowed his head ever so slightly—"I have some reason to be familiar with some practices of medicine."

When the prelate raised his head, Robert could see the humor in his eye. Had Isabel shown Scotland's leading clergyman the roguish poem he had written about quack doctors? "Then you think in Isabel's case—"

"That she's a whore? Use your eyes, man."

"Why then would she not protest her innocence?"

"Because if you could not see, would you be any better able to hear? No, you'll not find one like Isabel protesting her innocence."

The archbishop laid a hand lightly on Robert's shoulder and left him to meditate on those mysteries. Robert looked to the hill Scheves had first mentioned and tried to imagine the monument of his own. Might it be to one of the small people of the realm, an Isabel or an Ingram, for instance? It was doubtful. More likely to a great churchman, like Scheves himself, or to hero of the wars for Scottish independence, Robert the Bruce, maybe even William Wallace. No, the small people had to have their monuments carved into the heart of God.

The next morning Robert and George met to see Archbishop Scheves off. "There's no more that I can do," he told them. "But then, she's ready. I do not fear for her. The sisters know their business."

"And us?" George asked.

"You might read to her. I think that would bring her comfort."

Turning to Robert, the archbishop extended his hand. "Perhaps we shall meet again in happier times and you will treat me to more of your poetry. At the very least, please send me copies of your work. Your Cresseid and your 'treatise' on medicine long for other kin on my shelves."

Robert bowed to hide his blush. "May your Grace go with God."

"Aye, indeed."

With that, Scheves took his staff from his waiting companion and they began the half-mile journey into the burgh of Stirling, where the friar would become archbishop once more. He had other pastoral work to do, comforting the heartsick queen, who sheltered her children in the castle during her husband's humiliation.

Robert and George stayed on another five days, well beyond the time allotted to them by Prior Gerald. It was clear that Isabel would not survive much longer, and Robert took it upon himself to allow the mother and son to spend together that remaining time. She was too weary to speak much, and her breath came in gasps. So Robert and George read to her, as Archbishop Scheves had suggested, from the poetry of King David.

Shortly after he spelled George one evening, Robert turned to Psalm 44: "*Eructavit cor meum verbum bonum….*" He did not translate for Isabel. For one thing, she knew Latin even better than some of the abbey brothers. For another, he was not even certain that she was conscious: she had made no stir when he and George exchanged places. But he read on anyway.

This, a royal psalm in praise of the king's marriage, had inspired him throughout his life as a writer. Although he could not hope to match David's divine grace and passion, he had caught a glimpse of them.

> Fine words leap from my heart. I utter words I have crafted about the king. My tongue is a scribe's pen, busily writing. You are more handsome than the sons of men; grace is poured into your lips. Strap your sword upon your thigh, in your great power and with your glory and your loveliness; and in your majesty ride prosperously because of truth and mercy and justice; and your right hand shall teach you to perform great marvels.

As Robert read, he forgot where he was and became more and more agitated. What a contrast between this glorious procession and the recent events in his own pitiful kingdom! Overweening magnates, a king headstrong even in his weakness. Where was the loveliness or the mercy or the justice in events that withered and destroyed the lives and spirits of these young people who had been like sons and a daughter to him?

So carried away was he by this idea that he did not at first hear Isabel whispering the words of the psalm along with him: "*Audi filia et vide et inclina aurem tuam...*" Robert ceased. Isabel did not seem to notice but kept reciting, her eyes still closed. She breathed the words in shorter and shorter phrases as life ebbed from her:

> Hear, O daughter, and see; sharpen your ear. Forget your own people and your father's house. And the king shall greatly desire your beauty, because he is your Lord, and all will adore him....

At that moment, George came back into the cell. He was about to speak when he, too, heard Isabel's voice. "To replace the family you have lost, you shall give birth to children; and you shall make them princes in all the earth." She stretched out her arm to him, and he took her hand. "I will make your name to be remembered in all generations: therefore the people shall praise you for ever and ever, world without end."

As she spoke these words, Robert thought a kind of light began to emanate from her face, transforming her decayed features. For just a moment he could imagine a king greatly desiring her as he himself had once done. For just a moment he saw her enshrined by a royal monument on the hill overlooking the spital house. Then, just as suddenly as the vision came, it disappeared. Isabel was dead.

Robert leaned back on his pillow in his cell. He could not control his tears. In part, he wept for the waste. Scotland was never to see the Psalm fulfilled, at least not in his lifetime. Archbishop Scheves' efforts to heal the broken kingdom had been but a patch. James' brush with deposition had made him only more determined to tame the wild Angus and the magnates by sheer will, not by diplomacy. He became paranoid, suspecting even his queen and their firstborn, also named James; and they languished, estranged from him, in Stirling Castle until her death just shy of her thirtieth birthday in 1486. What the king sought to prevent, his actions had perhaps encouraged. The sentiment against him only festered, and the nobles wooed the prince to "lead" them. In 1488, the king was killed and

James, the fourth of that name, was crowned. All Scheves' work was for naught, and by that time he was getting too old to be able to exert much of a further influence. He died in 1497, to be replaced by James IV's brother, James, Duke of Ross.

But if Scotland were disappointed in its hopes, Robert was certain that he had caught just a glimpse of a glory even greater, the crowning of another queen of heaven. This was a joy to weep for. Isabel's transfiguration had lasted only the briefest of seconds. But as he neared his own death, it was this picture he now saw in his mind's eye—not the youthful loveliness he had cherished, nor the corruption that had so revolted him. His desire for her was now on someone else's behalf.

> Would my good lady love me best,
> This would I declare:
> I should, of virtues—the highest—
> Make her garments fair.
>
> Her shirt should bind her body round
> With chastity so clean
> And shame and dread together bound—
> How brilliant is its sheen!
>
> Her gown should be of goodliness,
> Well ribboned with renown;
> Purfilled with pleasure in each place,
> Furred in finest fashion.
>
> Her belt should be of benignity
> About her waist so small;
> Her mantle of humility
> To withstand wind and squall.
>
> Her shoes so sturdy should be formed
> That she in sin not slide;
> And honesty her hose so warm
> I should for her provide.
>
> Would she put on this garment true,
> I dare swear by my seal

That never cloth of green nor blue
Would set her half so well.

XIII

The Wolf and the Lamb

"**S**o this is what it is like to die?"

The end was soon. Dawn was beginning to break, and he hoped that he could hold out long enough for Charles to perform one last great act of fellowship.

Imagining death was nothing new to Robert. As a result of his temperament, perhaps, he had often reflected on the subject. Although the fact of death never really frightened him, the manner by which it operated did arouse anxiety from time to time. The plague, for instance, terrified him. The frequency and ferocity with which it struck. Its randomness, carrying off whom it would without warning, regardless of rank or the precautions one took. During one of the outbreaks, Robert had even composed a prayer for the pest.

> Have mercy, Lord, have mercy, Heaven's King;
> Have mercy of your people penitent;
> Have mercy on our piteous punishing.
> Retract your sentence and your just judgment;
> Against our sins thy anger's fully bent;
> Without mercy we may make no defence.
> Thou, that on the cruel rood was rent,
> Preserve us from this perilous pestilence.

138

Remember, Lord, how dear thou has us bought,
That for us sinners shed thy precious blood;
Now to redeem that thou has made of naught,
That is of virtue barren to renew,
Have pity on thine own similitude;
Punish with pity, not with violence.
We know it is for our ingratitude
That we are punished with this pestilence.

Robert had been spared the pest, though he had seen some of his acquaintaince taken off by it and often those the sturdiest. After a time, even that fear wore off. But what had seemed most frightening of all, more so than the plague or anything else, was the loneliness. He was not overly fond of company, except for the select companionship of folk like Charles or like Martin, himself now gone some twenty years. But that no one should come with him during his last voyage. The thought had been almost unbearable.

Now, as death was finally upon him, he realized that his fears were for naught. The new kingdom was growing ever more substantial to him; and though he longed for Charles usher him into the kingdom, it was as much for Charles' sake as his own that the longing arose. No, it was the living who suffered most from loneliness, not the dying. His life had been full of moments of intense loneliness...and never more so than in that summer of 1482, when most of what was dear to him was taken away.

After the events at Lauder Bridge, he was in a foul mood. Not even Charles was present to cheer him up. The cellarer was away in Edinburgh to meet a shipment of Burgundian wines. It was market day and business at The Lion and Mouse had long since passed the point of briskness. "Frenetic" was the more accurate word. With his ale and the promise of a meat pie, he threaded his way to the single unoccupied bench at the rear of the tavern, with his back to the bar. He sipped at the ale while waiting for his food.

At one point he became vaguely aware of a lingering presence behind him. Perhaps it was his food. A familiar voice spoke, "Is it as good as Father Charles'?"

He looked up to see John standing over him.

"Might I sit down?"

Robert turned his head toward a window in an effort to ignore him. John began to squeeze himself onto a bench between the wall and a farmer of massive bulk, the one nearly as immoveable as the other. Unable to contain his anger any longer, Robert turned to his former student and spat out, "You dare show yourself around here?"

"I'm doing well. And how are you?"

"Do not be so impudent."

John's face flushed. "I little expected such a greeting."

"What greeting could I offer you? The Earl of Angus must be well pleased he has at his disposal one whose tongue is filed so smooth."

"In what way did I err?"

"Can you not see?"

"Nay, tell me."

"That shameless account of events at Lauder, dripping with Angus' praise, with no mention at all of poor Ingram."

"What would you have me do?" John's tone was less a question than a protest.

"Tell the truth."

"And wherein did I not? You forget, Master Robert. I was there."

"Did Ingram try to save Master Roger?"

"You'll catechize me, then?"

"Just answer my question."

"Aye. Ingram made to save the musician." John's lower lip began to quiver.

"And did not one of Angus' henchmen stab him?"

"He raised his sword. I do not believe he intended to harm him."

"But Ingram fell by his sword."

"If you will insist."

"But I do insist—on the truth. And George made a move to save him and you did not even raise your pen."

"So that's what this is about. About George and me." John's eyes welled with tears, but he refused to let them overflow.

"You've sold your birthright, son, for a mess of Angus' pottage."

"And George has leapt in before me to claim your blessing. Is that it?"

"After all the hope I had in you. All that I gave you." Robert knew, as soon as he had spoken these words, that he had allowed his anger and disappointment to color his judgment. It was a serious error, and John's sharp legal mind would allow no retreat.

"All the hope that you had in me; all that you gave me. This seems less to do with the truth, sir, than with your own self."

"What do you mean?" Robert tried to recover himself.

"You know well what I mean, though little else. You would not soil your hands in the law. Hide in the safety of your schoolroom, instead, and lay the burdens on others' backs. Look at you. You're no better than that bullying Abbot Henry."

Robert's anger boiled over and he forgot himself. Lunging across the table, he struck John full in the face. The arm had long since lost its plowboy's strength, but the force of the blow was enough to drive the young man's head back against the wall. That corner of the tavern grew hushed, as men turned in surprise toward the respected schoolmaster and the stranger who was wiping blood from his bleeding lip on finery that bore the insignia of the mighty Earl of Angus.

It was John who spoke first. "I'm sorry. It was my grief speaking. I had no right—" He hurried to make his escape. The boisterous sea of men crowding the tavern calmed and parted before him. The servant, who had just entered from the kitchen with Robert's food, looked about him in wonder at the silence. He edged nervously toward the table. There he saw Robert, cradling his sore fist and rocking back and forth.

"Your meat pie, sir?"

For six years, Robert heard nothing from John. All letters sent to Tantallon Castle, home to the mighty Angus, evoked no reply. During that time, the animosity between King James and Angus and others grew even greater, despite the bloodletting on Lauder Bridge. More blood needed to be spilled, royal blood, for the nation to be healed of her deep sickness. War, that great leech, performed the duty at Sauchieburn, near to Stirling in June of 1488. By the end of the day, King James III lay dead and his son was crowned James IV. In early August, Robert at last received a short letter from John, urging him to come with some haste. Three days later, sped along by the Abbot's own horse, he arrived at Tantallon. Although under orders from the Earl of Angus himself to admit Robert, the jailer was surly in welcome.

"You've a half hour, no longer. The Earl's command."

"Then spend no more of it talking, man. Admit me."

The jailer snorted but was bound to obey. He clanged the key in the lock and pushed the door open. It squealed in resistance. The cell was dark, close, and fetid. It took a moment for Robert's eyes to become adjusted, and in the meantime he stumbled upon the chamber pot.

"For Jesu's sake, man, empty this thing."

"His lordship said nothing about tidying the room. Besides, tomorrow it will make no difference."

"Leave us." Robert could feel the jailer scowl, but again the man obeyed. The door was just as reluctant to close.

A figure lying on a mat in the corner attempted to rise but fell back. "It was good of you to come, Master Robert. It's been a wee while."

"Six years. And not a day's gone by but I've regretted our last meeting."

"That makes two of us, then."

Robert knelt beside the figure. With a ladle he drew water from a bucket by the mat. He smelled it and threw it down. He rose, strode across the cell, and banged on the door. "Another bucket of water." Some grumbling through the small barred window. "And fresh this time or your master'll hear about it." He returned to the cot. "They have not treated you well."

"Not so bad to kill me. They're saving that till tomorrow. Still, they had an impression to make before I departed out of the Earl's service."

"O John, my son. What happened?"

"The Earl's court found me guilty of treason."

"Treason?"

"Aye. It's rather complicated to explain. I would not fight with him against James III."

"But why wait till now to bring you to justice?"

"To see how the wind blew after Sauchieburn. If he did away with me before the king was defeated, then I, apparently, would be seen as a martyr. Since the new King James is on the throne, all that is forgotten. He can hang me, and seem to be doing justice—to make an example of me."

The jailer's assistant interrupted. "The pail of water you requested, sir."

"Is that you, Matthew?" John whispered.

"Aye, sir."

"Thank you for your kindnesses."

"I'd be a faithless servant otherwise. Will there be anything else, sir?"

"No," John answered.

"Whatever is in your power to make this man's last hours more comfortable," Robert added.

"Yes sir. My master's just gone to dinner. I'll see what I can do." The assistant bowed and, noticing the overflowing chamber pot, took it up and left.

Robert continued. "And there's no appeal to the king?"

"I am the Earl's man and subject to his laws. Anyway, the king would be glad to be rid of me. A guilty conscience, I should think."

John had served the Angus long enough to know something of the power of that lord's anger, and he had experienced it firsthand now. But although John's body was broken, his spirit was not; and he leaned back with a faint smile. In Robert, it was the heart that was breaking.

"What can I do for you, my son?"

"A prayer before you go, and a prayer tomorrow, and—" he paused.

"What is it?"

"Would you stay till the end? I would take great comfort to see at least one friendly face in the crowd."

Robert knew what a well-trained executioner could do. And a nobleman of Angus' stature could afford the best. Such a one could stave off death and protract suffering for a long time. Tomorrow was likely to be a fearsome display. Robert could scarcely contemplate it, but he could hardly say no to the pain of witness, when Isabel and Ingram and George and now John had suffered so much more.

"Aye, I'll be there." He leaned over and whispered a prayer. Then he kissed John on the forehead.

John closed his eyes and smiled. "Thank you, Master Robert. I'll sleep for a time."

Robert waited for a moment at his student's side, then rose and knocked quietly on the cell door so as not to disturb John's rest. The jailer's assistant opened it. Robert made to leave.

"A word with you before you go, sir?" the assistant whispered.

"What is it?"

"You're the condemned man's schoolmaster?"

"Aye."

"I was his valet, until the sad times, sir. His fall from favor rocked my wee boat, though mine did not capsize as his did."

"I'm sorry to hear of your troubles."

"I have Master John's example to steer my boat aright. But my own lot is of little concern."

"What is it, then?"

"He spoke highly of you, sir, and was ever grieved at your anger with him."

"He told you of that, did he?"

"Aye. I think there's something you ought to know, although he would never have told you."

"What is that?"

"I was at the Lauder Bridge when Ingram Bannatyne and the others were killed. In fact, I was serving Master John when Earl Archibald and the others planned the event."

Robert bit at his lip to keep silent.

"The Earl was in favor of sterner measures."

"Such as?"

"Deposing King James and placing the Duke of Albany on the throne. As the English did poor Richard II."

"And look what it's got them. Thirty years of civil war."

"That is precisely what Master John reminded the Earl, though in terms as tactful and persuasive as any I've heard. It was the king's life he wished to preserve; and if he could maneuver the Earl into doing so, he was not above casting the Earl in a more heroic light."

Robert marveled. This was an act worthy of his own master, William Cunningham. Still, he was not yet fully satisfied. "But what about the deaths?"

"There was certain to be a bloodletting. The nobles wanted scapegoats to appease their frustration. Master John was a lone man against so many."

"And Ingram's death? Why did John not mention that in his chronicle?"

"It was an accident. But if word got abroad that the magnates had killed indiscriminately, then the realm would be divided even more than it already was, and all efforts for peace would be undermined."

The servant waited for the words to take effect. He continued. "I can not tell you the depth of Master John's grief. He got the Earl's permission to bury Ingram in the chapel here at Tantallon and he's paid from his own pocket the chantry priest to say a Mass for his friend's soul once a month for these six years."

Robert turned involuntarily back to the cell where John was awaiting the end of his life…a course that he, Robert, had been largely responsible for setting him on and during which he, Robert, had in ignorance forsaken him. "God forgive me."

"I'm sure he will. Master John forgave you many years ago."

"Thank you, Matthew—"

"Forbes, sir. Matthew Forbes of Haddington."

"Then thank you, Matthew Forbes of Haddington." Robert pressed a pair of shillings into his hand.

"I will not take coin for telling the truth."

"Then take it to the chantry priest that he might say a prayer for the soul of a prince ready to enter the kingdom of his father and for a poor wretch unworthy to pave the way with his master's gown."

"Jesu bless you, sir."

The earl had made a point of not being present at the castle during this time, pleading business in Edinburgh. And certainly there was business enough to conduct. If the matter at Lauder Bridge, where the king's servants had been slain, required delicacy and tact, the death of the king at Sauchieburn demanded his constant vigilance. There was no telling how the new king might react. The life of a kingmaker was a precarious one, and Angus had no wish to share the fate of his English counterparts, the Percies and the Earl of Warwick.

Robert suspected that there was another reason the earl was absent: his fondness for John. For all his power, Angus, like others in his position, was at heart a simple man. That simplicity, governed by his one principle, devotion to himself, judged all other men by one standard: their loyalty or disloyalty. He could little understand the simplicity of a man like John, who was also governed by a single principle: devotion to another above himself. The earl could never understand that; thus, to him, all that John did or said seemed the intricate maneuverings of a subtle mind trained to be that way in the study of the law. It was much easier to remove John rather than to switch simplicities. Robert suspected that Angus would suffer for this great refusal. Robert had not understood John's simplicity and had paid a terrible price of his own over these past six years.

The next day John was brought forth. The dull, cloudy, August morning nevertheless dazzled him, accustomed as he had been to the darkness of his prison cell for the last two months. In the midst of the jeering crowd, Robert hoped to catch John's eye, to offer him the comfort he had requested the day before. But John had already set his face towards the kingdom he was about to enter, and Robert rebuked himself for what he recognized as a selfish desire: to be wanted where he was not needed. Thankfully, the Master of that kingdom was eager to welcome his servant into his presence; and before the skilled Phillipe Buchard made his first incision, John was dead. Robert bowed his head.

XIV

The Abbey Walk

As Robert had hoped, Charles did come, earlier than usual, as if led by some premonition that he was to lose his friend that day. Charles was followed by Abbot George, who carried with him a small box containing a chrism of oil, a miniature flagon of wine, the Host, and a silver paten and chalice.

"Robert?" Charles called out. "Are you awake?"

Robert nodded. It was about all he could manage.

Charles turned to George. "We've come none too soon." To Robert he said, "The good abbot has come to administer the last rites. It would seem that this world's physic has done all it can do and it's time to let the divine Physician have a go with you."

After the last rites, Robert held out his hand to Charles and whispered but one word, which was to be his last: "Eucharist." George beckoned to Charles to celebrate. In that tuneless voice, now creaky with age, Charles intoned: "The Lord be with you."

George answered, "And also with you." Robert mouthed the words.

After the collect, Charles sang, "And joining our voices with angels and archangels, we forevermore proclaiming thy praise with thanksgiving."

At that point, Robert began to cough. The death rattle was upon him. George and Charles accompanied him with the "*Sanctus*" even as he passed out of this world. They continued with the Great Thanksgiving and laid the Host, dipped in wine, in Robert's gaping mouth. "The Body and Blood of our Lord Jesu Christ keep you in eternal life," Charles whispered.

"Amen," George said on behalf of the still body.

Charles closed the open mouth and eyes, then finished the service. Afterwards, George collected the instruments of his profession and slipped out of the cell.

For a time, the old cellarer sat alone in silence, holding his friend's hand. There were no tears; he had long since prepared himself for the moment.

A sound of rustling at his feet stirred him from his reverie. A set of whiskers attached to a small gray nose was chewing on the corner of a piece of parchment lying under the bed.

"Och, away with you, or I'll let Augustina in, certain enough," Charles cried, and the whiskers and nose disappeared. He picked up the leaf. In a frail, spidery hand were these verses, at the top of which were written "The Abbey Walk":

> Alone as I went up and down,
> Through an abbey fair to see,
> By chance there fell upon my eye
> A message chiseled on a wall:
> "Of what estate, man, that thou be,
> Obey and thank thy God of all.
>
> "Thy kingdom and thy great empire,
> Thy royalty and rich array,
> Thy gold and all thy goods so gay,
> When Fortune wills, will from thee fall:
> Since thou examples sees each day,
> Obey and thank thy God of all.
>
> "Though thou be blind or have a halt,
> Or be thy face deformed so ill,
> So it come not through thy own fault,
> Spur not thy foot against the wall,
> But with meek heart and prayer still
> Obey and thank thy God of all.
>
> "In wealth be meek, puff not thy self,
> Be glad in willing poverty;
> Remember him that died on tree

For thy sake tasted bitter gall,
Who downward casts and raises high—
Obey and thank thy God of all."

When Robert had written the lines, Charles did not know. Tucking the manuscript under his arm, he left the room, taking care to keep the cat out.

Epilogue

Found among the effects of Reverend Matthew Inglis, pastor of St. Andrews Church, Edinburgh.

To the Reverend Matthew Inglis, greetings in the name of our Lord Jesus Christ.

You have inquired about the verse of Master Robert Henryson, tutor to Samuel Inglis, your great-great-grandfather, and to his sister, Isabel. Be pleased to accept this small labor from your humble servant, compiled in my youth during the time of the great reformation in our Kingdom. You will discover that it is divided into five parts.

Part 1. Those verses composed to God's glory and our salvation, in which is contained Master Robert's "A Prayer for the Pest"

Part 2. Those ballads full of wisdom and morality: Master Robert's "Abbey Walk" and "The Reasoning Between Age and Youth"

Part 3. Ballads merry: "Some Practices of Medicine"

Part 4. Those poems devoted to love: "The Garment of Good Ladies"

Part 5. The fables of Aesop with diverse other fables and poetical works: The *Orpheus*, "Robin and Makyn," the fables of Aesop the Phrygian, and "The Bloody Shirt."

The pieces came into my hand by way of my grandfather, Robert Bannatyne, steward to Lord Bothwell, son of Ingram Bannatyne, assistant choral master to James III, and godson to the same Master Robert. It was Ingram who set "The Bloody Shirt" to music in honor of our Lord and Savior. My grandfather claimed that they were a gift from Charles Braidwod, a priest at the Abbey of Dunfermline and confessor to Master Robert.

Your most obedient servant,
George Bannatyne

Dated this thirtieth day of January in the year of our Lord 1602,
the thirty-fifth year of the reign of our blessed King James, the
sixth of that name.

Found among the effects of George Crichton, a manuscript containing
this colophon:

"This manuscript was compiled by me, John Asloan, notary public,
at the request of George Crichton, beloved abbot of the convent
of Dunfermline. Containing certain poems of Robert Henryson,
schoolmaster of the said convent: choice fables of Aesop the Phrygian concerning a toad and a mouse and the trial of the fox; the
Testament of that most pitiable lady, Cresseid of Troy; and lay of
Orpheus. The *Testament* and the *Orpheus* were bequeathed to him by
his mother, Isabel Inglis of Stirling.

Dated this second day of October in the year of our Lord 1506 in
the royal burgh Dunfermline.

Printed by Walter Chepman and Andrew Myllar, licensed by royal pat-
ent of King James IV, a tract containing the *Orpheus* and "The Lack of
Wise Men," commissioned by George Crichton, Abbot of Dunfermline.
Dated the fifth day of May *anno Domini* 1508.

About the Author

John Craig McDonald lives in Blountville, Tennessee, with Karen, his wife of nearly thirty-two years, and with three cats and two dogs. Their daughter, Kate, and her husband, Justin Reynolds, live in the Borders of Scotland, not far from Crichton Castle. Their son, Seth, works in Cincinnati. For most of the last twenty-five years John has taught at King College in Bristol, Tennessee. Presently, he directs the Snider honors program there. His hobbies are reading, writing, gardening, and watching British mysteries with Karen. He has recently completed a second historical novel, *An Early Fall*, this time on the Battle of Flodden.

John's interest in the Scottish Middle Ages in large part grew out of his heritage. A descendant of emigrant Scots from the 1760s, he studied the poet Robert Henryson while a doctoral student at the University of York in England. His scholarly publications include articles on 15th-century Scottish literature and history and an edition of a medieval religious handbook, *The Meroure of Wyssdome*, published by the Scottish Text Society in 1990.

John has also written poetry, largely pieces centered on events from the Gospels. A short cycle of these poems was set to music by the composer Kenton Coe. Another piece was published in *Sojourners Magazine*. Yet another is to appear shortly in the newly launched arts magazine *Haven's Grey*.

Of his novel *Among His Personal Effects*, McDonald states: "Twenty-five years of teaching medieval and Renaissance literature has given me a profound respect for the great richness and complexity of this age, so that, although the story in many of its details is fictional, I have tried very hard to remain true to the spirit of this period in Scotland's history. I have also tried to capture something of what I have discovered about being a teacher, to see one's great aspirations for his or her students bent, broken, or refashioned by the terrible grace of Providence."

You may write the author at: **handsel3031@yahoo.com.**

Printed in the United States
130214LV00005B/9/P

9 781602 900202